How to Leave Hialeah

The

John

Simmons

Short

Fiction

Award

University

of Iowa Press

Iowa City

Jennine Capó Crucet

How to Leave Hialeah

University of Iowa Press, Iowa City 52242

www.uiowapress.org

Printed in the United States of America

The University of Iowa Press is a member of Green Press Initiative and is committed to preserving natural resources.

Printed on acid-free paper

ISBN-13: 978-1-58729-816-5
ISBN-10: 1-58729-816-3
LCCN: 2009923717

For Andrew

Resurrection, or: The Story behind the Failure of the 2003 Radio Salsa 98.1 Semi-Annual Cuban and/or Puerto Rican Heritage Festival / 1
El Destino Hauling / 11
And in the Morning, Work / 26
The Next Move / 42
Animal Control / 63
Noche Buena / 69
Low Tide / 87
Men Who Punched Me in the Face / 101
Relapsing, Remitting / 116
Drift / 136
How to Leave Hialeah / 153

Contents

ACKNOWLEDGMENTS

This book exists only because of the generosity and all-around awesomeness of the following people and organizations: Curtis Sittenfeld, Holly Carver, Allison Thomas, and everyone at UI Press, the Bread Loaf Writers' Conference, the Department of Spanish and Portuguese at UC-Irvine and their Chicano/Latino Literary Prize, Miriam Altshuler, Jake Nabel, Don Lee, Jan McCrae, Julie Wakeman-Linn, and Joseph Levens. Thank you to the following magazines for first publishing earlier versions of these stories: "Resurrection" in *Ploughshares*, "Noche Buena" in the *Northwest Review*, "Animal Control" in the *Potomac Review*, "And in the Morning, Work" in the *Summerset Review*, "The Next Move" in the *Southern Review*, "Relapsing, Remitting" in *Crazyhorse*, "Men Who Punched Me in the Face" in *Gulf Coast*, and "How to Leave Hialeah" in *Epoch*.

Much love to the writers Helena Viramontes, Lamar Herrin, Charles Baxter, David Treuer, Luis Urrea, Margo Rabb, and Patricia Engel, for their insights and encouragement on these stories. À la the Grammies, I'd like to give a shout out to God for his many blessings, American High's Class of '99, P.S.N. Elementary's Class of '92, the City of Hialeah and the rest of the 305, Cindy Cruz, the M.E.A.N.H.O.E.S. of Wyckoff, the Cornell Skitsos of yesteryear, my mentees at P.N.G., and all the haters out there—like Tupac, I've got nothing but love for y'all.

I cannot even begin to thank my ridiculously amazing and inspiring family—the Capós, Crucets, Santanas, Missels, Valles, and all the other crews—for their love, prayers, and faith, and for teaching me to rely on all three. I owe you guys everything. A special gracias a mi Abuela Celaida, la cuentera en nuestra familia, por lo mucho que sacrificó para sus hijos, y por lo mucho que ella habla. Thanks to my sister, Kathy, for being my first audience and the inadvertent victim of my first attempts at writing. Thank you to my parents, Chary and Rey, for their patience with me, and for their love. And finally, thank you to my best friend and husband, Andrew, for his ursine love and steadfast nature, and for believing in this book more than I did.

How to Leave Hialeah

Resurrection, or: The Story behind the Failure of the 2003 Radio Salsa 98.1 Semi-Annual Cuban and/or Puerto Rican Heritage Festival

The church is quiet except for the nun's approaching footsteps. You could imagine the sound of the soft soles of her shoes scuffing down the center aisle, coming toward the last pew, barely growing louder as they approach. Or you could imagine that someone has just finished playing an organ, practicing before the morning Mass—is it really only four, didn't it feel like the sun was about to come out?—the notes echoing off the high ceilings and moving into silence. You could imagine the church's entire frame rattling from the distant boom of the bass beat at a nearby dance club. Any of these will work fine.

Hidden in the candlelight of hundreds of prayers sits Jesenia, whose face seems solemn, though she didn't bother to cross herself or kneel. Her halter top is bluish-silver, hanging from her neck and made of a material that ripples like a bothered puddle when she breathes. The blouse is dark under her arms, and her hair sticks to her still-damp forehead. You decide she must have come straight from Shadow Lounge—she still wears a paper wristband, and she winces when she swallows. She closes her eyes as if to hear the leftover bass from the dance floor; she traces an imaginary line up and down the length of her arm, and frowns. The only thing left to decide about her night up to this moment: acid or Ecstasy. Maybe both—from the way she rubs her jaw muscles, she could have been candy-flipping. A friend of yours might have tried this once, probably at a club; he claimed it made him see people's faces melt off and their souls (which he described as looking like Slimer from *Ghostbusters*) pour out through their eye sockets.

The nun is not at all old, and that makes sense; of course a young nun—in her mid-twenties maybe, not much older than Jesenia—would be in charge of these early morning hours, when drained young people were most likely to stumble in. The nun reaches Jesenia's pew and sits very close to her, so close that her habit presses into the girl's bare shoulder. These two might know each other, you can see; perhaps they were close friends before either received any sort of calling. Jesenia keeps her eyes closed, puts her head on the nun's shoulder, and offers her the arm to stroke, but the nun does not move.

The church is empty except for these two women and the candles behind them.

—I was rolling, two pills, Jesenia says. I'm checking, but it's gone.

She slumps further against the nun. A car starts outside the church doors directly behind them. She barely turns her head to listen for it—her ride there, you imagine, a beefy boyfriend with earrings who shaves his arms. The engine's grumble fades away.

—I told him to leave me here, don't worry, Jesenia says. Sister, I need to ask you a favor. Her throat pulses with another dry swallow. She says, It's about my job.

The nun slides away from her on the pew, and from the way her eyebrows carve closer together, you change your mind; the nun has never before this moment seen Jesenia.

—Where do you work, mi hija?

Jesenia juts out her lips as she runs her tongue over her teeth. She probably tastes chalk—she wrinkles her face at the tang of it. She does not answer the nun, but stands and walks to the arched entrance of the church. She cups her hand and says, I'm so totally sorry but I'm freaking gonna die if I don't. She leans down, drinks from the holy water.

The nun might have rushed to stop her, but her eyes are soft with understanding, so she only stands and steps forward. You can see from the way she bows her head to stare instead at the mosaic of tiny tiles encrusted in the floor that the nun lets many thirsty people drink when the church is empty. This church is too close to South Beach, and like the clubs, it's open all night. And like the clubs, the water is free. But here, at the church, there is never a line.

Jesenia is barefoot, her feet blistered where straps from heels have cut into them. You can see smudges of dirt on her ankles and shins. She wipes water from her mouth.

—Tell me how to bring someone back from the dead, Jesenia says.

The nun does not move. Maybe she thinks the Ecstasy is still working its way out of the synapses of the girl's brain. Or she could be troubled by these kinds of questions, and the kind of people who ask them. But when the still-thirsty woman crosses her arms over her chest, looking down to make sure she's covering the cleavage she'd so forcefully propped up earlier that night when she'd squeezed her breasts together in front of her bedroom mirror, you see that it is Jesenia who's troubled.

—Where do you—

—My bad, Jesenia says. I work at Radio Salsa 98.1. I have an internship—they don't pay me or nothing. I got it through my cousin, who knows a guy who goes part-time to Miami-Dade Community College. He'd heard about it.

Jesenia looks down at her feet, at the bright red polish on her toes, magically still intact. She begins to wiggle them and says, I need to bring somebody back from the dead for work, to get a promotion.

The nun seems to snort from her nose, as if she were a small bull. You can't tell from the sound if she's amused or angry. She crosses her arms to match Jesenia's, but Jesenia frees hers, letting them fly as she tells the nun what she might have told anyone in any other church anywhere else in Miami had her boyfriend taken a different road home from Shadow Lounge.

—I swear I'm a good person, Sister. It's just, between school and this job—where I don't even get paid!—sometimes I wanna get torn up, feel like more than I am, and that's why God gave us weekends, and Ecstasy. And I'm sorry, but it's *not* like coke because it is mostly natural and not addictive. Except that you wanna feel that good all the time—it's not the chemicals that do that to you. Like you with God, but I'm not giving my life to it, though seriously I respect all this church stuff like crazy—my mom baptized me and I even got confirmed.

This is how these pookie-heads talk; you know that; even the nun knows that.

Jesenia must have wanted the nun to nod, because here she stopped until the nun did just that. Then Jesenia swallows hard and smiles widely, showing a row of perfect but caked-on teeth. They're covered with such a thick yellow film that, if you could, you'd reach through the page and brush them for her.

—Which is why God brought me the idea to raise Celia Cruz from the dead for this concert I'm promoting.

The smile vanishes, the crud back in hiding, much to your relief. Jesenia takes a step toward the nun, whose mouth is twitching as if she might laugh, or maybe spit.

—Because me and Jorge were at Shadow Lounge, and I'd taken two DGs, like him. In the middle of this trance set, the deejay cuts in with this remix of Celia's *La Negra Tiene Tumbao.* And I swear on my grandfather that is not dead that the beat and her big hot voice came up through my legs, and up into my chest, and right into my heart, Sister.

Jesenia has put her hands at the tops of the nun's arms. She curls her heavy-knuckled fingers into the black robe, pulsing them into what you could imagine to be the buttery tops of the nun's ham-hock arms, moved only at the beginnings and ends of prayers.

—Jorge sees me smiling and starts to massage my neck. The trumpets in the song match up perfect with the lights trailing like a freaked-out rainbow, and I'm so happy I start thinking I might fall down, and then it comes to me—and it's hard to hold onto stuff when you're rolling, so I know God wants this—that this happiness is something everyone has to feel, Sister, and that Celia Cruz needs to come back to bring it to them at the Radio Salsa 98.1 Semi-Annual Cuban and/or Puerto Rican Heritage Festival, which I, as an intern who does not get paid, was put in semi-charge of organizing. Because she's only been dead a couple months, and I think if we pray hard enough it can happen.

The nun grabs Jesenia's hands, jarring her from the trance of her own voice. You wonder if she's still rolling, figuring she might be, a little. The nun's short nails cut into Jesenia's wrists.

—This is not God's work, the nun says.

Jesenia pulls her hands away from the nun's grip, rubs her wrists, crinkling the paper band.

—I'm trying to *fix* something, Jesenia says.

She raises her arms over her head and starts tying the long rope of her hair into a knot. She says, It's a *good* idea. I *have* ideas. You're just pissed about how I got it, which I understand, seriously, I do. But still, please help me bring her back. Something that big will definitely, without a doubt, for sure, probably get me a real job at the station.

The nun says again, shifting her voice and her eyes, This is not *God's* work.

The nun lifts her eyebrows and stares at Jesenia long after the sentence has been left there, and then Jesenia figures it out—even if you haven't yet, but you're sure you will soon—and she nods and says, very softly, Oooh. The nun leans over to the pew and removes a white card tucked into one of the programs for Mass. On the blank side, using a small, blunt pencil stored somewhere underneath her long robe, she scribbles the address of a santera.

—Ocila might help, she says, handing the card to Jesenia. *Might.* Take her una ofrenda of a hundred and fifty dollars. Put the offering in a white envelope tied with a red bow. Take her flowers, any kind, as long as they are white—all the way white.

Jesenia puts the card in the waistband of her skirt.

—And tell her hi from Marcela her sister—her *Sister* sister—and that I say to stop smoking those unfiltered cigarettes, la loca. She already sounds like a man with that voice, and I no am interested in having now a brother.

Jesenia nods at all of this. These are the kinds of practices she's been raised not to believe in, but nonetheless respect, because of the time her mother took her to a santera to undo un trabajo that her mother thought was causing Jesenia's acne—she'd come down with her first period the day after the visit.

Jesenia grabs her shoes from the pew and says, Thank you thank you thank you. She kisses the nun on the cheek and says as she runs out, I'll tell you if I get the promotion. As she leaves, Jesenia crosses herself, moving her hand too fast to register what you notice—that she does it in the wrong order.

You're not sure how she gets there—and with all the requisite supplies no less!—but you care only vaguely about these questions. You go with it, you figure *what the hell*—and there's Jesenia at Ocila's santera table, which squats in the middle of her bedroom, too close to the bed to feel like a separate space. On it is a small seashell-framed placard that says *All sales final—aquí no hay 'refund.'* They sit facing each other, the table between them. Jesenia's back is to the television, which is still on, but muted—Ocila killed the sound not after taking the money, but later, when Jesenia mentioned Marcela's name.

Ocila is a hefty woman whose neck ripples when she talks, her voice as rough as the nun had suggested. Her thick brown hair sits on the very top of her head in a bun so perfect it looks like a plain donut. You would guess she was almost forty years old from the flower print housedress and straw-colored cardigan she wears, but she must be younger; there is a photo on the wall of the narrow hallway that leads back to her bedroom, or her *office* as she calls it, of Ocila next to the nun (the former wearing a robe, but not a nun's one) at what looks like a high school graduation.

—Okay, so I telling you now, Ocila says, that I can no control lo que pasa. Especially this early in the morning. I can no say your santo will no be mad at you for waking him up.

She stops here, probably waiting for Jesenia to say she understands the terms, but she—Jesenia—is looking around the room, frowning. A half-finished bowl of cereal waits on the nightstand, turned to mush. The walls are ivory, and she sees no candles or statues perched in the corners. The ceiling fan is still, and from each blade dangles a thick cord of dust. You could say the room, even the whole townhouse, seems more regular than any room in any townhouse you had ever seen, except for the oddly placed table and its little frame, and a jar full of pennies and feathers on the floor propping open the bedroom door. So you reason that maybe santeras don't necessarily like advertising their religious affiliations through their home decor.

—Señora, Jesenia says, if you don't mind, how long you been doing consultas like this?

—Eh? Cómo? Many, many times. And yes, I am minding. Okay.

Ocila smoothes the red tablecloth with her palms, her rings thumping against the wood underneath, her gold bangles crashing into each other. Without the TV, and with the day barely started outside, you'd think it was the only sound for miles.

How many consultas, you think, does one need to perform to acquire the kind of money that buys so much jewelry? But then you see them (Jesenia doesn't notice), the bands of skin turned green at the base of each of her fingers. The rings aren't real gold—they're fake.

Ocila finally says, So. What is your problem that you come to me like this?

She gestures with her noisy hands to Jesenia's halter top.

—I wanted to see you right away, she says. Before I forgot, and before I figure out I'm probably wrong.

She is coming down hard now, the cereal on the nightstand rocking her stomach. She can barely feel her legs and she is sticky with sweat. She wants water almost as much as she wants it to already be next Friday.

—Can I have some water, please? she says.

—You no come here for water, Ocila says. Her eyes flick back and forth to the TV. She clutches the edge of the tablecloth in her hand.

—Right. So, I need help with something for my job which is actually just an internship.

Ocila's grip loosens on the tablecloth. She sits back in her chair and rests her hands on her belly.

—Okay, work related? Very, very easy. For that we no even need the flowers you bring.

Jesenia puts her palms flat on the table.

—I need you to bring Celia Cruz back from the dead to do one last concert.

Ocila pushes back from the table with both arms. Then she crosses herself three times, the last time kissing her own hand. At first you assume that she's thinking of her very holy sister Marcela and suddenly feeling guilty. But what you don't know is that santeros actually do believe in and pray to God, to Jesus, to the Virgin Mary. It's just that they have *alternatives,* these other spiritual connections that they can consult should the heavy hitters turn a blind eye your way. You can think of them like religious bonuses, like a 1-Up in a video game.

—Ay Dios mío, Ocila says, That is a very different thing that you say.

Ocila looks at her lap and grabs the underside of her chair. She scoots closer in, then back out, then back in again, so close that her breasts spill onto the table between them. Once she's pressed herself into the edge, she brings her hands up and uses just the middle finger of her left hand to scratch at various spots around her head, spots right underneath the bun. Jesenia winces at the sound of so many rattling bracelets. Ocila clears her throat over and over again, then presses the same middle finger into her ear and begins wiggling it—as if trying to get at a deep itch—while making a hacking sound. Even Jesenia can see that Ocila is stalling.

She clears her throat twice more and finally looks back up at Jesenia.

—Bueno, chica, I have to tell you, is no gonna be easy, and you see my sign, I no do money back guarantee.

You knew Jesenia's money was gone almost as soon as she'd walked in the door, from the way Ocila had folded the cash and tucked it into her bra, the strap snapping the money in place. But still, Jesenia hopes for a miracle, so she nods.

—Okay, Ocila says.

She clears her throat again, then readjusts the cardigan on her sloped shoulders. Her eyes are huge, and her chest rises and falls so quickly that the gold cross lashed around her neck looks as if it's about to launch itself toward the ceiling.

—Let's begin, she says.

What happens next is up to you because it relies on your knowledge of Santería. Maybe Ocila mashes the flowers into a paste and smears it on Jesenia's upper lip while playing *Celia Cruz's Greatest Hits* on a loop. Maybe she makes a powder that Jesenia must then sprinkle over both Celia's grave and the stage where she wants her to perform. Maybe she spreads chicken feathers on the ground and has Jesenia lay out on them while Ocila douses her with sugar water.

The point is, barring your own attempts at research—and you know how lazy you can be, how else do you find the time to read stuff like this?—you need to be *told*, preferably by someone you'd consider an expert, an insider. Someone who knows enough to drop the name *Changó* (a.k.a. Santa Bárbara) or *Babalu-aye* (a.k.a. San Lázaro) in the same way Ocila does to give her act credibility in front of Jesenia. Maybe your narrator—me—then tells you about the santeros that lived across the street from my childhood home. How one morning, I woke up to find our entire driveway covered in pennies. I tell you how my mother made us all—my father, my grandmother, my two sisters, and my younger brother—pee in a bucket so Mom could pour it over the pennies and sweep them out into the street to undo the trabajo they'd done on our house for only Changó knows what reason. I might admit that that's pretty much the extent of my firsthand experience with Santería. Your narrator, however, thanks God for such ignorance.

But what kind of story would such a confession leave you with? Not the one you expected—you wanted chicken blood, people wearing burlap, goats maybe, statues eating fruit and drinking bottles of beer. You want zombies. And Jesenia—she just wants something real to happen, and she fools herself weekend after weekend into thinking that she is a VIP. She just wants to forget that she can't stay behind the velvet rope come Monday morning.

But here's what happens: Jesenia watches Ocila heave herself around the room, chanting to the ceiling, and after twenty minutes of this, when absolutely nothing has happened except Ocila suffering a coughing attack midway through, she figures out she's being ripped off. She realizes—just as you are, reading this—that

Ocila cannot really do what she claims to do for a living; she can't conjure spirits, she can't make you hear voices, she can't convince you to believe in something you don't trust. Jesenia then leaves the room—she abandons her shoes, feeling too stupid to ask Ocila where she'd put them—and she walks down the block, ignoring the rocks scraping the soles of her feet.

She makes it as far as the corner two blocks down, where a car—a brand new Mitsubishi something or other with the windows rolled down—is stopped at a red light. You and Jesenia recognize him as another member of the Beautiful South Beach Weekend Elite (maybe he bags groceries during the week, maybe sells sneakers in the mall; of course he still lives with his parents). He's heading home from a night (then morning) of dancing, pimping, and random Ecstasy-encouraged massaging. His music plays so loud that the entire frame of the car rattles on the chassis.

Jesenia knows the blasting salsa remix. She puts her arms over her head and starts to dance, right there on the corner, the sun barely up. The driver has just received a text message containing the directions to the after-party's after-party—we won't be attending—and because he's looking down at his phone he never sees Jesenia's hips grinding against a NO PARKING FROM HERE TO CORNER sign. The light turns green and her fellow *Yo-bouncer-I'm-on-the-list* velvet rope clinger spins his tires, but even the scream of the car peeling out doesn't overtake his system's bass, or the clear, robotlike voice of the singer. Even when the car is blocks away from her, Jesenia still feels the song, and she figures she has nothing better to do, nowhere to be, so she keeps dancing, the memory of the music enough to last her all the way to next weekend.

And you, you keep watching her, hardly believing people like this exist.

El Destino Hauling

I was raised to think of Tío Nando as just that—an uncle, part of that huge group of men who grew up with my father. When I realized that I also called his son, Fernandito, Tío, I asked my father how they could both be my uncles. I was eight then. My father fumbled with the domino stand in front of him.

—What do you want? He's my uncle, he's my cousin.

He pointed to the balding man shuffling dominos—Nando—then to the one with the dark ponytail. I felt confused and so kept staring—how then were they *my* tíos? He refused to look at me and instead paid a lot of attention to the dominos lying face down on the table, waiting to be chosen. In picking his ten, he got the double zero, but his face betrayed nothing to the others.

Still studying his fichas, he finally said, They're nobody to you. But he said it in English—a language he never learned to trust—which made me doubt his answer. Also, he'd had a couple beers because, as Nando had yelled into our answering machine that afternoon, we were celebrating: Fernandito and Nando had just moved in together after being kicked out by their respective wives. The woman who kicked Nando out, Linet, was not Fernandito's mother; *that* woman had stayed in Cuba, had kicked Nando out close to ten years before I was even born.

Much to my mother's fury, I spent most of that night by the domino table instead of on the screened-in porch with her and the other married-in family members. I remember hanging on the table's edge, my fingers curled beneath its plastic top, watching my father and my various tíos christen the new apartment with toasts and marathon domino games. Aside from my cousin Ileana, who was four months older than me and therefore cooler than my sister Nuria, and my Tía Maribel, Ileana's grandmother and Nando's sister, I was the only girl inside, my face so close to the beer bottles that I could see each individual bead of water tremble its way down the sweating glass.

Nuria, having just turned five, was too little to escape from my mom's lap and join us inside. I watched her watery eyes through the rust-rimmed windows, and I knew my desertion would earn me her back that night, that she would not face me as we slept side by side on the sofa bed. I even thought of leaving the table, since back then I'd already started having trouble falling asleep and usually had to make myself drowsy by counting her long lashes or the number of her breaths. But the men had started a game and were now slamming the dominos down, numbers-side up, and the clatter made me turn back to them, to Nando's broad hand pushing his piece in place.

Nando brought the dominos with him from Cuba, having bribed an official during his exit inspection not to take them from him. They were made of real ivory, but had yellowed over the years, so much so that they reminded me then of butterscotch candies. I remember wanting to grab one and take it home to show to Nuria later and win her back, but I knew better than to try and touch something so many men found so valuable.

It was at that domino table—hours after my mother gave up trying to make time-to-go eye contact with my father, then with me, from her spot outside—that I first heard about the Dump Truck Plan. Going into that night, it seemed to me common family knowledge that Nando and Fernandito made their living through various schemes, usually insurance fraud. Fernandito's wife, it turned out, actually left him because she refused to be part of yet another slip-and-fall case. She was tired, he told the other men, of having to do groceries in a neck brace. Fernandito had funded his late twenties and early thirties with car insurance scams; people who for whatever reason wanted to get rid of their cars would arrange for Fernandito to "steal" them, then he would take the car someplace, strip it for parts, and set it on fire. In return, he got a third of the insurance money and whatever he got for the parts. Nando introduced Fernandito to this line of work, having done it himself until he hurt his back ripping out the passenger seat from a Thunderbird.

Someone asked Nando why his wife left him this time. Maribel, hovering over the domino table with her hands on her hips, answered for him, yelling, Ella se volvió loca, como siempre. Nando did not confirm or deny his sister's ideas about his ex-wife's sanity. He only made a shushing sound so low that I think only I heard it, and he whispered, Ya, hermana, ya. Enough already.

On her fingers, Maribel started to list Linet's offenses against the family.

—She tried to make my brother—my *own brother*—swear he would not come over during the week anymore. Like he can't get liquor at the store. And *I'm* low class? In Cuba her mother used to piss in the middle of the road like nothing. Everyone in town called her Squats.

My cousin Ileana watched Maribel and rolled her eyes. Bor-ing, she mouthed, then abandoned her spot by the table. She shuffled away—her grandmother's rant about esa puta Linet being old news to her—and flopped down on the couch behind us, pushing her hands between the cushions in search of the remote.

—I have an announcement, Nando said suddenly. Everyone stopped laughing and turned from Maribel to him.

He told us that he and his son planned on making a legitimate go at the business world—no more scams. The Dump Truck Plan was something he'd been thinking about for a few months, when things with his second wife started to look like they'd eventually explode for good. Now that he and his son were roommates, he saw no reason why this partnership shouldn't extend to a financial endeavor, and based on Fernandito's sleepy, drunken nods, it looked like he agreed. Eventually one of my other tíos waiting for his turn at dominos told him to get to the fucking point already, and so Tío Nando winked at his son and obliged.

—Here it is, he said with a domino in each hand. We buy a dump truck. This is the initial investment, okay fine. Then we start a business. What is our business? Moving things *with* the dump truck. What things? Dirt, sand, rocks, things like this, right? We move dirt, sand, whatever—*with* the dump truck—from places like construction sites to places like trains. And vice versa. People—all kinds of people—*need* these things to happen. People are gonna *pay us* to make them happen.

I waited for someone to start laughing, for Tía Maribel to swoop by and smack the back of his head with the stiff towel she was using to wipe up spilled beer. I waited for my father to finally acknowledge my devoted presence with an eye roll. But none of these things happened. One by one, my tíos lifted their eyebrows, pushed out their lower lips, looked at each other, their faces saying, Not a bad idea. Soon each person at the table, along with those hovering around waiting to claim spots, was slowly nodding his tilted head.

Fernandito stood up, his folding chair scraping the linoleum, a fresh bottle in his hand. Ileana turned away from the TV to watch him. He said, almost crying, My papi is one inteligente motherfucker.

This pronouncement was followed by some cheers, some happy grunts, some backslapping. Maribel put her hand on Nando's shoulder and squeezed it so hard her knuckles were white. One tío said, Bueno chico, me suena bien. Another said, Yeah, sounds *too* good almost.

But my father made what was to me the most shocking comment of all. He scooted his chair just a little bit further away from me and said, Best part? You don't have your wives to get in your way, trying to stop you.

My mother and the other still-around wives could not believe it, but Nando and Fernandito survived their first week. Then their second. They hadn't burned down the apartment complex, or gotten evicted because of the noise they made, or starved to death. Maribel had only had to come over to break up one fight, and when she got there and separated them long enough to ask questions, neither could remember the reason the argument had even begun. Anabel, who was Tío Fito's wife and a santera, claimed to have put the evil eye on both Nando and his son the night of the party—as payback for what those two put their wives through, she said—but as far as everyone could tell, it hadn't worked.

On the Thursday of the third week, after a lunch of arroz imperial purchased by the pound during which they'd started brainstorming company names—the best two, they thought, being AAA Hauling (because they'd get the first spot in the phonebook) and El Destino Hauling (which just felt right)—they bought and brought home the dump truck. Fernandito drove, having driven one before because of an insurance job on a similar vehicle several years earlier, while Nando sat in the passenger seat, complaining about a banging noise only he heard, something sounding not right with the tailpipe. The truck took up both of the parking spots assigned to their apartment and blocked more than half of the neighboring apartment's front window. They knew they'd have to find a better place to park it, but they didn't think they'd have to do it so soon: the super, an old Puerto Rican lady they'd seen walking barefoot up and down the concrete stairs of the complex, called within the hour to tell them about several just-made complaints.

Fernandito was the one who got the phone, figuring after the fifth ring that his father must be in the bathroom; Nando had spent the second half of lunch silently farting and laughing when the scowls from people at neighboring tables landed on Fernandito instead of him. It's the ponytail, Nando had explained. Makes them think you're dirty.

Fernandito grabbed the keys from where they hung, on a slanted nail he'd pounded in by the front door. He slammed the door shut behind him, cursing the neighbors in a voice so loud it made them peek out their blinds to watch him. As he hoisted himself into the cab and started the engine, he could see his neighbors' fingers poking through the slats, their noses pressed against the glass. Just as he put the truck in reverse, he thought he heard someone yelling his name, but decided in that second that he must be hearing things; how could these neighbors know his name if he hadn't introduced himself to any of them? The truck roared beneath him, and he backed out quickly, without even looking, hoping his attitude would scare those spying on him, would make them afraid of messing with him again. He thought it had worked, too, when he saw the couple next door burst out their door and run screaming out of their apartment, their arms raised over their heads, their mouths wide open, into the space his truck had just left. He even laughed at their hysterics, at the way the woman covered her mouth with both hands and at the man grabbing her and turning her face away, until he backed up far enough to see for himself his father, the mess of meat, of blood.

I heard this and other versions at the funeral two days after what came to be known as *the accident* by some in our family, *the murder* by others. You would think that for a relative, the closer the blood ran to Fernandito, the less likely they'd be to think he did what he did on purpose, but it turned out to be the exact opposite with us. My mother thought we should visit him at the police department before going to the funeral home, take him some food, make sure the officers were treating him okay. My father did not want to align himself with his cousin; Maribel had handled the initial arrangements—what funeral home to send Nando to, what time the twenty-four-hour viewing would start—and had told my father not to give this information to Fernandito or Linet, should they call. What no one knew yet, though, was that a nurse at the hospital where they'd first taken Nando (he was dead by the time the ambulance arrived, though one version of the story has him saying his last words—supposedly, *I'm all fucked up por 'dentro*—to an EMT) had already contacted Linet because she was still legally married to him. Which meant of course that it was Linet who'd dictated what happened to Nando's remains. The nurse had told Linet only that Nando had been hit by a truck, and not knowing that he'd been run over pretty much from toes to face by both the back and front wheels, she'd insisted on an open casket viewing.

—His face is not really—presentable?—Señora, the nurse had said into the phone, but Linet cried that she would pay whatever she had to pay to see her husband one last time.

We arrived at the funeral just as Tío Ricky and Tío Fito hoisted a cooler into the trunk of Fito's Buick Regal. We parked two cars down from them.

—Ese comemierda told us no beer allowed, Fito yelled toward our car. He was talking about the funeral director. We're in fucking mourning here, he grinned as he held out his arms to embrace my dad. He wore a salmon-colored polo shirt. Wet patches spotted his armpits.

Fito squeezed and rocked my father for what felt like a long time. My sister and I pressed next to each other, swathed in identical black dresses—the ones we wore to church and to school awards assemblies. We were still close to the same height then; this was long before Nuria became The Tall One. Fito loosened his grip a little to give my father a huge kiss on the cheek. He made a smacking sound with his lips as he did it. His face over my dad's shoulder was damp and only a little red. My mom crossed her arms over her chest and said, Hola Fito.

But Fito, spying us there so close to the ground, came for us instead. He dropped down to his knees and put a hand on each of our outside shoulders, hugging us like we were one wide child. He kissed each of our foreheads, his heavy, bitter breath hitting me as he leaned in. The wetness of his mouth made my brow feel, for only a moment, cold.

Ricky was still by the cooler, sobbing. Unlike Fito, Ricky was wearing a suit. My father wore a tie and a dress shirt, having given in to my mom. I don't care what your cousins wear, she'd yelled at him as she pulled my dress down over my head. She'd just finished ironing it and still had my sister's to do.

Ricky plunged his hand into the cooler and brought out a dripping can of Budweiser, soaking his suit's sleeve. He walked over and flung his other arm around my dad's shoulder. He opened the can with the pointer finger of the same big hand in which he held it. It let out a hiss, and Ricky started crying again.

—Luis, he sniffled, Nando was my *uncle*.

He dug his face into my father's shoulder and cried harder, holding the open can far out from his body.

Fito stood to hug them both, and my mother used that as her chance to scoot us past them and into the funeral parlor.

Compared to the funerals I'd already been to and would eventually attend, Nando's looked like a fairly typical scene, except that my sister and I were the only children wearing dress clothes. The others were dressed as if they'd just come from school or daycare, which was probably the case. The place had at least a dozen mismatched couches tucked against the walls—an oversized living room with a coffin at one end. Maribel stood near the front, by the casket, wearing a knee-length black skirt that looked shorter in the back because of her huge behind. Her blouse was circus red with quarter-sized gold buttons shining down the front. She wore gold sandals with turquoise beads threaded on the straps. Her feet looked swollen in the shoes, but nuggets of hard, white skin seemed to protect the places most likely to become blisters. The room was loud, but I could hear her above the noise—her husky voice, yelling at a group of mourners about how her brother Nando looked like so much shit.

My sister and I were well trained and so had started our rounds without being told to do so. We went to each couch, from relative to relative, said Hola or Buenas, and kissed each person on the cheek. If they were old, we touched their hands as we leaned in to kiss them. I knew their faces, but I didn't know how we were related, not really, not anymore: I was still chewing on the fresh knowledge that Nando had been my tío for years without ever being my uncle. I remembered my father's words at the domino table halfway through our hellos, and when my mom noticed me slowing down, she pressed closer, herding us toward the next face.

Eventually we were presented to Maribel, who stopped midsentence to kiss us and my mom. But after that formality, she kept raging about Linet to a cluster of people—some of Nando's neighbors—as if we weren't there.

—Esa puta doesn't have the balls to show up here. And good for her, because all I want for my brother in his death is the respect esa puta never gave him when he was alive.

She dragged her thick fingers under her eyes, but there weren't any tears to wipe up. My mom nodded as if she were part of the conversation just as Maribel shifted her weight to nudge us out.

We were eventually allowed to go sit with Ileana, who was sprawled out on the carpet playing with a Game Boy. She wore a pink T-shirt and jeans with glittery swirls painted near the bottoms and on the butt pockets. She barely noticed us in front of her; her thumbs were still moving, the buttons clicking, when she said, I like your dresses.

—Thank you, we said in unison, which made me wish that Nuria would leave and go back with my mom, who was scratching at the back of her arm and half-slouching just outside of Maribel's circle.

—Are you guys staying all night? I have to.

She nodded her head in Maribel's direction.

—I don't know, I said.

My mom hadn't packed our pillows in the trunk, so my guess was we were not, though there was a decent chance that my father would go home and get them for us once we looked sleepy. I now realize that this is something my parents probably discussed ahead of time, but Nando's funeral came long before the era when they felt they needed to explain their decisions to us. Ileana pressed pause on her Game Boy and let it dangle in her hands. I could almost see my reflection in the screen—the lopsided ponytail, the crinkly poufed-out sleeves of my dress.

—You know what? she said. My mom says that one time, in Cuba, they buried some man who wasn't dead, but they *thought* he was dead, but he wasn't. And the man, he sat up right when they were closing the coffin and everyone freaked out. So because of that is why people wait all night until morning to bury dead people. In case they made a mistake. Which my mom says is stupid to still have to do because now when they think you're dead, they drain your blood and take your brains out through your nose, which *has* to make you dead even if you weren't before.

—Is your mom even *here*? my sister said.

Her voice surprised me, because usually she waited for me to talk before speaking herself. And she'd said it with a scowl, jumping on Ileana's words, and without reaching for my hand. I knew Nuria didn't believe her, that she thought Ileana was lying, that she wanted grownup verification of the story. Maybe what Ileana said scared her, but with her hands on her hips and her head tilted down at my cousin on the floor, Nuria looked more like an angry mom than my baby sister.

—What's *that* supposed to mean, Ileana said. Yes, she's *here*.

All three of us raised our heads and looked around for her. She'd recently dyed her long hair very red in an effort to get a permanent spot in a local hotel's lounge show. Her stage name was Maya, but her real name was Maribel, like her mother. Being short girls who would eventually grow into short women, Ileana and I were back then only at hip level to the adults, so finding Ileana's mom meant weaving our way around loud knots of people and looking up. The room was full enough that I got lost among the circles. I remember feeling the same kind of panic I had felt the few times I'd gotten separated from my mom while shopping at Zayre, a now long-gone store that sold overstock clothes and random household and personal items minutes away from expiring. My mom shopped there exclusively because it was the only place we could afford, but also because Zayre had given her father his first job—a night janitor—after coming here from Cuba. One time, as I was playing inside an extra densely packed circular clearance rack, I mistakenly thought I was trapped inside—I couldn't find the hole I'd squeezed in through, could no longer hear my sister's voice behind the thick ring of cheap long dresses. I felt something slick by my feet, and when I looked down, I saw my flip-flop pressing on a tube of toothpaste, the top of my other foot covered in coils of bluish gel. Only then did I scream, and within seconds my mother loomed above me, her hands pushing apart the wall of dresses long enough for her to order me out and to the section selling paper goods, where I was to find a half-open pack of napkins or toilet paper and wipe off my foot.

I bumped along the hips and butts of talking adults and came to an empty place near the entrance to the parlor. I had lost my sister and Ileana somewhere behind me, so I was alone when I saw her—Nando's wife Linet. She lingered just outside the doorway, thin and dressed all in black. She'd clearly been crying. Her burnt-blond hair was down but picked up on the sides, showing off how badly she needed her roots touched up, and a fringe of fried-looking bangs brushed against her chocolate-colored eyebrows. She was folding a piece of paper in her hands while looking down at the floor, which is why I was the first person she saw. I'm sure she didn't remember my name just then, but I knew hers, knew right away who she was. I thought of the shock of toothpaste on my foot, the minty cold slapping and sticking against my skin. But this time, screaming for my mom would not work; half the people there were moms, and yelling *Mami* would either make all or none of them turn around. And I didn't know if I even wanted to yell, if I even should—was I ready to be The One Who First Saw Linet for the rest of my life? Maybe, I thought, it would make me like Ileana, who seemed to not have a Dad's Side. She had only one abuela, only Maribel. Standing between Linet and the rest of us, I had—or at least, I thought I had—the chance to prove I was more than anything else my father's daughter, that half counting as a whole.

Linet must have noticed my furrowed brow, my clenched fists, the way I silently moved my lips, talking to myself, because she tilted her head and smiled at me. Her mascara smudges, I could tell, had been tended to before she'd come in, but the black began bleeding down again, filling in where she'd just cleaned up. Her lips looked like pieces of dried fruit, wrinkled yet full of something. Then her smile broke and she lifted her fist to her mouth, crying into it. With her head down even further now, I could see the gray hairs sprouting like wires from the base of her bangs. Clear snot began to drip from her nostrils straight down to the carpet and she did nothing at all to stop it. When she faced me again, the drops trickled down to her mouth. I imagined the salty taste. I knew for sure then that I wanted no part of her. In a voice so loud it easily matched Maribel's, I yelled, She's here.

Ileana magically appeared by my side, and I saw my sister emerge from another cluster of people for only a second before they turned toward me, pushing her back behind them. I thought Linet would stumble away, knocked back by my huge voice, but instead she cried, *Nandito!*, then leapt forward, charging through the crowd toward the coffin. I lost her immediately. From the other side of the parlor, I heard Maribel booming, Keep her away! Keep her the fuck away!

—Oh shit, Ileana whispered. She sounded just as scared as me, but when we faced each other, she was, to my complete shock, beaming.

—Let me see him, I heard Linet yell.

Ileana grabbed me by the wrist and hauled me through the bottom halves of our relatives. We came out at the very front, standing at the edge of the area cleared out for the fight. Ileana's mom stood at one end of the coffin, her red hair swaying behind her. I couldn't find my own mother anywhere.

Maribel had her sister-in-law by the head, her nails digging into Linet's scalp. She whipped her around and away from the casket, and people shifted back to make more space. The older relatives still on the couches grumbled that they couldn't see, so some of the standers near the front crouched down or dropped to their knees.

Her hand still tangled in Linet's hair, Maribel said, How could you tell them to open the box like that?

The skin of Linet's face was yanked back so tight that her eyes barely looked open. She said, I wanted to see him again before—

—Before what? Maribel yelled. He's already dead. Seeing him now changes anything? Go ahead and look.

She pushed Linet toward the casket. The spray of flowers near the other end of it trembled and almost fell off. Ileana's mom caught it as it slipped and pushed it back in place with her shoulder.

Maribel crossed her arms over her chest and said to Linet's back, You won't even recognize him. It's not my brother.

Murmurs of agreement came from the couches. Ileana nodded, and I did, too, even though neither of us was tall enough to see inside on our own. I stood on my toes and only saw the tip of Nando's nose. When I stepped forward a little more and pushed up a second time, harder, wanting so bad to see what Ileana had somehow seen, I felt a hand clamp on my shoulder and push down. The fingers curled into my skin, pressing deep behind my collarbone. I winced from the nails cutting into me, but I willed myself not to look up and back, not to risk seeing my mom telling me, through clenched teeth, Time to go.

This is what I did see, having one of the best views in the room: Linet yelling her husband's name over and over again, Maribel rolling her eyes. Linet throwing her right leg over the casket, then clutching its creamy inner lining, hoisting herself on top of the box. Her flailing limbs trying to keep her from slipping off the slick laminate like so much panicked swimming. Ileana grabbing a fistful of fabric as all three generations of Maribel united to pull at Linet's skirt, her black pantyhose suddenly exposed and shining with the strain it took to cover the expanse of her drooping ass. Linet's skirt finally tearing, the rip making some laugh, others gasp, and almost all draw in closer. Her falling, her desperate grab for Nando's face as she fell. Maribel's husky scream. Nuria's hand, wet from tears, suddenly on my other shoulder, her throat exposed as she looked up and her voice pleading, Mami, I couldn't find you.

This is what I would have seen had my mother not right then grabbed us both by the neck, twisted us around, and dragged us in the opposite direction, past my father, now at the back of the room, yelling, Where are you going, and getting no answer: Maribel and Linet whaling on each other. Tío Ricky making his way between them but only holding Maribel back, so that Linet got in some payback punches before Maribel's daughter pinned Linet's arms behind her back and sat on her, knees to shoulder blades. The funeral home director calling the police and apologizing for having to do so—*I have no choice,* he said. My father, an hour later, seeing the empty parking spot and calling the police officer over—*Oye! While you're still here*—before remembering that his wife had brought her keys with her.

I learned all this that night, just after the lights of the taxi that had brought my father home shined through our living room window and onto the sofa bed, where I was still up and busy boring holes into Nuria's back with my eyes. My father let himself in the house quietly, passing right by us and only slightly bumping the bed's corner on his way to the bathroom. After that, he went into the room where he and my mom slept, closing the door behind him. Seconds later, a light dimmed on, and I could hear my mom whispering. My father filled her in on what we'd missed, his voice getting louder and louder as he got to the part about the police, about thinking the car had been stolen. She shushed him every couple sentences, but he ignored her. I didn't know then that he was trying to wake us on purpose, to make my mom angry, to get back at her for leaving him. I thought, as I lay there tugging the sheet away from my sister, that he was talking to me *instead* of my mom, that someone had told him how I'd been the first to spot Linet. I thought he was telling me the end of the family story I'd started for us.

The mortician had tried to reconstruct Nando's face with wax, but no one had given him a picture to work from—not Linet, not Maribel, and certainly not Fernandito, who had been released from custody in time to arrive the next morning, just before the burial. My mother and father went back to see Nando buried; Nuria and I stayed with my mother's parents. I am told Fernandito did not cry over his father's grave, which is part of the reason some in the family still argue his guilt. Yet Linet's waterworks are what convinced these same people that she never loved Nando as much as the rest of us did.

The wax used to rebuild Nando's face was peach colored, but his skin was very tan, so his face in death looked as though patches of sunlight shined on it from some nonexistent window. He'd been buried smiling. We had the makeup artist to thank for that: she'd painted on new lips. Linet's attempt to climb into the coffin left Nando with a perfect handprint on his forehead where the wax caved in from the pressure of her fingers. Maribel tried to undo it, but she only made it worse; there was no way to get under the wax to pop it back out again. She shut the coffin to keep anyone else from seeing, but my mother had stood on her toes and seen, over Maribel's shoulder, Linet's perfect palm, then Maribel's frantic fingers digging at her brother's face.

The few times a year I see my father's family now, when I hear people tell the story of Tío Nando's death and funeral, they never mention me seeing Linet first. They never say, And then Patita yelled. They never even say, Then *someone* yelled. They never mention her desperate sprint toward her dead husband, her dripping nose, the wet spots she left on the cheap funeral home carpet. In their versions, Linet magically appears by the side of the coffin, Maribel's hand already in her hair.

Of course they never mention the handprint. They didn't see that either.

I always meant to tell my mom about that moment between me and Linet; it would have been a way to ask her what, in the end, she regretted. When my father died—an almost inevitable heart attack, an open casket, Maribel long gone and sent off with a funeral of her own—I half expected that moment to replay itself:

my mom showing up in tears, meeting my eyes, ready to face the wrath of the women who hadn't left my father. Maybe that would have happened had those women not also been her daughters. In this version, I'd made the arrangements, and Nuria had taken care of getting his suit. And unlike with Linet, we knew my mom was coming—we'd even left a message with her husband saying that she should call us if she wanted one of us to pick her up.

It was at my father's funeral that she told me about Linet's handprint. She'd kept that moment from me until that day, when, as we stood together by his coffin, I felt her begin to shake, and over the next few minutes, as I forced myself to imagine my father's sewn-shut mouth living forever on my face, she calmed herself just long enough to betray the memory responsible for making her laugh.

And in the Morning, Work

Marielena thought she'd arrived early enough at the cigar factory to prevent such a thing, but again she found Niño sitting on the stool from which she read to the rollers—his legs open wide, feet flat on the floor, trying to take up her space. Several magazines sat on the rolling bench in front of him. Marielena recognized the covers and frowned. *Bohemia,* a favorite of the island's masses, was *not* her idea of literature, but she had expected this kind of revolt ever since her first day as the lector at La Fábrica de Tabacos Francisco Donatién. Niño slid off her stool and stood in front of the other cigar rollers seated in rows at their dark wooden benches, their chests hidden by the shelves that housed their supplies. Niño gestured to the magazines with a sweep of his arm, bowing low in the old traditional way he was used to, as if introducing her to some important political officials.

—Niño, she said. She'd started as the factory's reader a week before, but Marielena still didn't know his real name, only that the other workers called him Niño because decades earlier, he had been brought in to work there by his father, who'd trained Niño as his own replacement. She thought it was a terrible nickname; she guessed he was at least twice her age.

—Señorita, he said, I bring you these. He bowed again, his arm still extended.

A few of the rollers in the front rows clapped their hands at Niño's presentation of the magazines. Marielena knew that he was smiling at her, the wrinkles around his mouth coming out more than she wished they did, so she kept her eyes on the floor. She could tell by the bits of waxy brown leaves pressed into the rough tile that the room had not been swept the day before.

From the pile of magazines, she knew that the workers did not think she was doing a good job as their reader. She had an audience of almost two hundred—mostly men, but also a few gray-haired women—and many of them had already offered suggestions regarding what she should bring in, as well as what she shouldn't bring back.

On her first day, she had tried José Martí.

—Ay Dios, por favor, someone said when she started reading. Other people laughed and someone coughed. A few of the younger men—those in their thirties and forties—rolled their eyes. Niño smiled and said, We're not in school anymore.

He followed that with a wink, the wrinkles around his eyes strangely unmoving like the veins on a dry leaf. His lip curled up to show his straight, storm cloud–colored teeth. She felt so embarrassed she almost let the book slip off her lap, and she scrambled to grab it before it fell. He looked back down, still smiling, and she shifted on the stool, pulling on her skirt for no reason. She pretended to look at the book to find the page she'd been reading from, but she was really looking at his workbench, at his browned hands pulling tight on leaves. He seemed younger than he was a moment ago, and she felt dizzy sitting on the tall stool at the front of the room.

The workers spent a lot of her first day as the lector interrupting her to recite different Martí poems—the easy ones they'd been forced to memorize for school plays decades earlier. So many of them knew "La Rosa Blanca" that they recited it in chorus, each worker joining in when the poem floated up from their memories. They pointed to the person next to them, wagged their fingers up and down with the rhythm of the poem's lines, closed their eyes and smiled as they read the words off some faraway page. She forced herself to laugh along with them as they recited. The long white room, with its maze of cigar benches, looked like an overgrown, smoky classroom. The laughter seemed to point at her, at her poor choice in reading material. The workers passed that long shift arguing about the edition she read from and joking about how she was too young to know what Martí *really* meant when he wrote about a white rose. The older women shushed the others before their own rose descriptions got too graphic, but the men defended themselves by saying, Just a little joke, mujer. She's a big girl.

At the end of that day, Niño placed the cigars he'd rolled in the wide, shallow cedar box near the center of his bench.

—Today was good, no? He grinned, his hands sliding over the smooth tubes of tobacco. She just shrugged, nodded slightly, and pressed the book to her chest with both arms. He raised his eyebrows and gestured at the book with his chin.

—Maybe tomorrow, something a little different, he said.

Now Niño placed his hand on her lower back and her head jolted up from the magazines to turn and look behind her. His hand drifted away from where it had just been, like he couldn't abandon her body just yet. The hand hovered there, and without looking at him, she knew her face was only inches from his. She worried he'd notice her fast breathing and take this as some sort of encouragement.

He motioned with the lingering hand for her to sit on her stool. From up there, she could see all the way to the back of the factory, though she could only watch the cigars being rolled in the first row, where Niño sat. During her breaks from reading, she would stay on the stool and sip water, pretending not to watch him pull the leaves from the damp stack to his left. He'd smooth each one out slowly, using only his middle and ring fingers, so that the leaf waited for him flat on the table. Then he would wedge his knife's wide blade into it, rocking the curve of the metal into the thin flesh of the plant. Underneath his steady hand, each piece came to have the tapered shape of a cigar. She always wondered how he was able to pull each leaf taut enough to roll the cigar tightly without ever ripping a single one.

Before taking his own seat, Niño slid the topmost magazine onto her lap and slapped it twice, softly, with a flat hand. When he did this, she felt the weight of the pages press against her thighs.

So she read the magazines during the morning, and in the afternoon, at the older men's requests, both newspapers, *La Granma Internacionál* and *La Granma Diário*. ¡Noticias! they cheered when Niño suggested it—like the news was the guest of honor at a party and had just arrived. He stood up and bowed then, too, first toward the rest of the room, then to her. He sat back down when she picked up the paper from the bench, then he waved victoriously to those behind him.

He tried to walk her home at the end of the day. Of course she refused; she was shocked he even attempted this after the magazines, after *noticias*. Only then, with her angry *No,* did Niño understand that the magazines were not appreciated. She thought he deserved the snub after an entirely wasted day reading about the speculated scandals of the Spanish monarchy, and about how bodies, bloated and shark-bitten, floated inland off the north coast—a day not full of literature but of written garbage and Niño's waves.

He grabbed her shoulder as she turned away from him and said, We like you.

—You like *Bohemia,* she said. She hid the book she'd brought but hadn't read, *Love in the Time of Cholera,* under her arm, hoping he wouldn't notice it.

—Today went fast. You don't think? he said.

Marielena made fists at her sides. She said, I don't need to think, do I?

Niño smiled and looked down. Only when they stood this close together could she see the little beads of lice clinging in clumps to the roots of his thinning hair. She almost explained to him that he shouldn't smile, that she was being mean to him, on purpose, that she was mad about the magazines, and that he was supposed to roll cigars, and she was supposed to read while he rolled them. He was *not* supposed to be standing so close that she could see lice and wrinkles; close enough to see everything wrong with him.

—Okay, he said finally, almost laughing. Okay. But let me walk *with* you at least.

Most of the other rollers had left already, except for some very old men still on their way out and hunched over from their day at the bench. When they said goodbye, Niño pushed his shoulders back so that he stood painfully straight and said, Until tomorrow, you old horses. Until tomorrow, boy, they laughed back.

Niño held out his arm for her, hooking it and cocking his head toward her. He laughed a little and said, Come, I'll even carry your magazines for you.

She turned on her heel, terrified she might cry from anger, and that he would mistake it for a different kind of sensitivity. She pushed past the old men still filing out through the heavy wooden doors that led to the street.

—I will try again tomorrow, he yelled after her, but she didn't look back. On the walk home, she worried about whether he'd meant bringing more magazines or asking her again about walking home.

After work, she went to the library to find the right book. She greeted the librarian, tall at his bench, with a nod. He looked sleepy behind the stacks of books, all folded into each other, open to the cards glued on the insides of the back covers.

At La Universidad de La Habana, she'd studied to be a librarian, but the lector position was the best the school's job placement counselor could offer her upon graduation. Taking the job meant leaving the capital's paved streets for Pinar del Río, a much smaller municipality about a hundred miles southwest.

—There is no work in libraries available at this time, the counselor had said as she handed him her transcripts and the other necessary forms required of those hoping to work in the university library system. She remembered his glasses sliding down his nose, his face twitching frantically to push them back up, his nostrils determined to do that work without bothering his hands for help. He was old, and ugly, with too many hairs between his eyebrows, the bridge of his glasses resting in that patch. A dead gray shadowed the skin where a beard could be, and her smile went unreturned when she first sat down in front of his old desk. His ugliness had made her sure from the moment she sat that he was going to say, *There is no work*, no matter what forms she showed him.

—We have this, he'd said.

He placed her papers in the desk's lower drawer—she never got them back—and he slid the notice of the lector position in the cigar factory to her side of the worn desk, pushing it with two stiff, widely spread fingers, not looking at the form at all, and not really at her, either. She had hoped this wouldn't be the case, but had been warned it could be. She tried not to cry or ask questions that would make her sound angry.

—This is with books, he'd said. She'd nodded.

The cigar factory in Pinar del Río could hire her right away—the counselor called and confirmed this in front of her—and it paid the equivalent of twenty-two U.S. dollars a month. That would be enough to send some to her mother—she could not see dragging Mamá away from La Habana, so the money would have to be wired—and she would not have to use any of it to buy the books to read from, as these were promised as part of her job, though she only received access to the literature, not ownership of it.

She walked past the shelf that held books on reserve for her. These she had selected the week after she'd moved to Pinar del Río, before her first day. She'd found the library disappointing—there were nowhere near as many books as there had been in the university's collection in the capital. She wrote about this in a letter to her mother, but had not heard back from her yet. She regretted, now, putting the complaint on paper.

Marielena knew she did not have much time to search for something new; her last rooster, which she kept hidden in the room she rented, was used to her being home before the sun was completely down. She worried that varying the rooster's routine would make him noisy enough to be noticed. She'd heard the smaller towns in Cuba worked like this, everyone always watching everyone else, always listening. And she hadn't yet figured out who on their block was on the Comité—it seemed there was no way to know here.

In La Habana, the people who worked for the Comité de la Defensa de la Revolución were proud; they would come into Mamá's home, sometimes even weekly, and take inventory while Marielena made them café, if they had the water and the coffee. The neighborhood official looked into the kitchen cabinets, made sure they had the right amounts of food legal for two women—one over fifty—and no more than that. During the day they hid their roosters and chickens under wooden crates at the bottom of a bedroom closet, the doors lined inside with thick sheets to keep in feathers and the scratching sounds of claws on tile. The neighbor in the Comité would gossip with Mamá about the fantastic things she'd found in other houses—an entire side of beef, a gallon of whole milk, a copy of the *Miami Herald*—and Mamá would say, ¡Ay, Dios mío! Where could they have gotten that? Incredible what people try! And the Comité member would tell Mamá, Trust me, they are paying for it now, and drink the café. Mamá would laugh—she was so good, sometimes even Marielena couldn't tell if she was faking it or if she actually found the stupidity of her neighbors hilarious. Together, her mother and the Comité member would marvel at how the younger generations seemed to be lacking fierceness in their loyalty. They'd discuss the first, most exciting years of the Revolution. Mamá would distract them with stories of Marielena's work at the university, and they'd comment on what a fine daughter she'd raised, how a daughter like that was a *real* thing of value, something that deserved more attention from the community than contraband milk or beef. They'd have such a good conversation that the Comité member would leave with just a glance in the direction of the closet, clearing her throat as they passed it, and then talking and laughing throughout the rest of the inspection. Looking underneath the bed that the mother and daughter slept in, the Comité member would say, People just don't *think*. You know where I found that *Miami Herald*? By a toilet!

But Pinar del Río, as far as Marielena could tell, treated the Comité like a secret. She wondered if her block even had one; some mornings it sounded like every home for miles hid a rooster. In her short time in the community, she'd noticed that it seemed okay to hide things—something about the effort made it excusable. But she didn't know this place well enough, and a misplaced evening crow worried her more than her book choice. She left quickly, leading with her chin as she walked through the tomb of books, purposely not wishing the librarian good night. She left the library with nothing.

When the rooster's crows woke her the next morning, she immediately regretted not picking out the book the night before. She sat up, rubbed her eyes, and watched the bird dash under the bed, back toward the cardboard box that held some of her books. Her own library was sparse—she laughed for even using the word *library* in her head—filled with the few books that had made it through the package inspections. They'd been sent by cousins in the U.S., family that had fled after the Revolution. She hardly remembered them, she was maybe three when her uncles had left—her own mother, and so she too, deliberately staying—and their long letters listed books that should have been there but weren't. She couldn't really be disappointed; she had never heard of those authors anyway, though their names sounded like neighbors she could have had. The classics always made it through all right. But the books she'd studied and loved in school during her librarian's training were not the kind the cigar rollers wanted to hear her read from; she'd already read the workers some of what she owned, and what she hadn't read them she knew they wouldn't like. After the failure of Martí, she'd tried Neruda, and she thought it had gone well until near the end of that day, when a leaf smashed into a lumpy ball bounced off her chest and landed between the book's open pages. She'd heard a muffled snort from the middle of the room when she paused her reading. They hadn't enjoyed poetry as much as she thought they should, but Niño had looked up from his work the moment she'd stopped reading.

One leg dropped heavy from the thin mattress, her foot smacking the floor and sticking to the muddy tile. She pushed her hair off her forehead.

—Ay Dios mío, she said, and the other leg followed. She leaned back on her arms, her palms flat against the mattress, and yawned. It was already hot though the sun was barely up. The room glowed a dark smoky purple. The rooster pecked at the floor where the tile almost met the wall at the corner farthest from her bed. The rooster still had most of his light brown feathers despite his poor diet. Each violent prod of his beak into the corner's dirt sent tremors through his bent tail feathers, so that she thought he might shake one loose with every stab. She felt a queasiness that she blamed on hunger, though she knew it was more likely her nerves; she had never gone to sleep without having the book picked out, waiting for her on the chair, on top of her clothes for the next day.

She sat on her bed thinking of the top of Niño's head when he'd bowed to her the day before, and this thought finally forced her to stand. I will find *something*, she thought, I can't—reading *Bohemia*—I won't.

Her bare thighs pressed on the tile as she squatted to sit cross-legged on the floor. She pulled the torn cardboard box out from underneath the wire frame of the bed. She lifted the folded blanket that covered what was inside, doubled it again, and slid it under her to pad her bones. Before looking through the books in the box, she yawned again and scratched her head. Her fingernails came back with oily black flakes underneath them. She ran each nail between her bottom and top teeth, scooping the grit out to clean them, and spitting it off the tip of her tongue. She listened to the rooster—still scratching at the corner—while tasting dirt and ash. The granules made her teeth feel rough.

The mornings in Pinar del Río were filled with a quiet Marielena found frightening. In La Habana, noise started early: buses, people laughing while sitting on their steps, even the distant ruckus of the ocean. Something about knowing that thousands of people had already woken up around her made it possible for her to do it herself. But she hadn't adjusted to the silent starts of Pinar del Río; cries from roosters shut up in houses began the day here, and not bus engines on the sleepless boulevard below her old window. There were no streetlights creeping away with the sunrise like there had been in her small apartment in La Habana. The first night in the room she rented in Pinar del Río, swamped by a quiet so profound that her ears rang, she marveled at how her hands disappeared in front of her face in the bedtime darkness.

Her stomach growled, and she decided to eat before looking through the books. There was some meat left in the small refrigerator from the other rooster, the one she had killed almost a week ago. That rooster's feathers had been falling out anyway, and Mamá had insisted when she decided to take them with her that the things were for eating—that she eat them before they got sick or killed each other. Marielena had grabbed that rooster by his head and spun his body in a tight circle. She had felt his neck crack in her hand, a series of pops registering in her palm, but she'd heard nothing. She had plucked the few feathers that still hung off his body, boiled him, and pulled the thin strips of soggy meat from the bones.

The last bit of this sat in a bowl in the refrigerator, covered with a wet towel. She held the bowl now, pressing the towel to her mouth to check if it was still damp, then she dropped it on top of the small fridge as she stood and walked back to the cardboard box. The rooster ran from the doorway—he seemed to have been watching her—across the room to his corner. He spread his wings far out from his body, like a woman holding out elaborate skirts to keep from stepping on them. She wondered whether, when she killed him, the sounds from the neighbor's roosters would be enough to wake her.

She picked at the gray rubbery meat and sat on the bed again, looking down at the books. The magazines Niño had brought to work had been too much; she needed something good. She wouldn't give him the chance to embarrass her again. She worked the food over in her mouth, moving the mush around until it formed a little ball. The sun was brighter now and she could read the spines of the books from her place on the bed. Their covers were worn, all of them paperbacks. The letters in the packages from her cousins had explained that hardcover versions, with their extra weight, cost too much to send from Miami. Most of the books she'd received in school—the few she'd been allowed to keep—were hardcover. She always felt lucky to have these. Most were gifts given in secret from her university instructors, proof she'd been an excellent student. She kept them out of the box, displayed on the little shelf above her bed next to a framed picture of Mamá (thin and young and alone, in her wedding dress), a stiff cardboard picture of La Caridad del Cobre, patron saint of Cuba, and another picture—very faded—of Baby Jesus.

There were other things in the box whose value gave her reason to keep them under the bed and covered. There was a bar of soap, which she had been saving for some time. The box read "Zest," a word she didn't know and had never said out loud. She could smell the perfume of the bar through the box, had held it to her nose for a long time the day she got the package, breathed it in for so long that she worried she'd spend it all somehow. She knew that the family in the U.S. must have sent at least ten other bars like it in order for that one to be left by the government's inspectors. She had wrapped it in a clean T-shirt, thinking that would help it stay fresh. She hoped to use it someday when she knew a man would be so physically close to her that smelling like perfume and clean would really matter, would even be necessary to keep from being embarrassed.

There were some Kotex pads, and these she stored underneath everything else in the hidden box because they were valuable, but also because they could humiliate her. Each month during her period, she would try to make each pad last overnight, but usually couldn't do this on the first or second days because these were her heaviest. She'd make up for the necessary waste of using more than one by trying to go without them at the end of those weeks; the brown spots staining her underwear were worth making the pads last.

There were other things, too: a manila envelope that held all the letters from the packages; an unopened bag of women's razors; a picture of one of the uncles who had left in a military uniform; a plastic bag filled with cotton balls—she was saving these because the pads would eventually run out; a bottle of rubbing alcohol; three rolls of toilet paper; a shoebox full of unopened packages of different sized batteries.

She reached down into the bowl with two fingers. It was empty, so she reasoned that she was a little less hungry.

She could not put Niño's stack of magazines out of her mind even as she scanned the titles of the books on the shelf. One near the middle caught her attention. Propped up against the framed wedding picture stood *The Motorcycle Diaries: A Latin American Journey,* the first of Che Guevara's books that she'd read while still in high school. It had been years since she'd opened it, but she remembered the fights, the parties, the serious drinking: things that had made her and her classmates read on, stories that had filled their talk at lunchtime. Yes, she thought, it was the kind of thing that would keep the workers interested, but even if it didn't, they'd think hard before complaining because it was Che's book. They'd understand; the respect for him ran deep for generations. And no one would ask for anything else, fearing that such a request would be taken as a much more serious statement.

She leaned across the bed, the sheet a crumpled ball beneath her stomach, and slid the book off the shelf. She left it on the bed while she dressed. She wore the same skirt as the day before, the one with the large yellow flowers, but she slid a white cotton shirt over the tank top she'd slept in. She hoped it smelled clean enough.

At the pedestal sink in the corner, she picked up the mug sitting upside down on the ledge. She bent down and lifted the towel covering the water bucket and dipped the mug into it. Water had not been coming in regularly to Pinar del Río for many years. Back in La Habana, there had been a few hours on some days when the water would come straight from the sink, a luxury she missed now that she lived in this tobacco-farming town. Some homes in Pinar del Río got their water from wells, but most depended on the water trucks that came every week or so in the afternoons. The cigar factory closed during those times, if they had advance warning, so that the workers could go home to fill buckets.

She spooned ashes from the pot next to the bucket into the mug and sipped, swishing the thick water around in her mouth to clean her teeth. She spit into the sink, directly into the drain, so she wouldn't have to waste water to rinse out the basin. This made her think of Mamá, because she had taught her this trick.

She sipped and spit until there was no more water in the mug, then she dipped it in the bucket again and drank.

She stood in front of the mirror and inspected her face, greasy around the nose and forehead. Her cheeks were rough red patches, with scars from pimples streaking them like blush. She pressed her cheeks with the tips of her fingers and watched them turn a different, darker red. She leaned into the hallway and grabbed the damp towel that had been covering the chicken and scrubbed her face with it. It made her feel a little cleaner. She ran a comb through her thick black hair, which was so oily it held the little grooves left by the comb's teeth—perfect, chunky rows. She patted the crown of her head, smacking away the gray clumps of dandruff. She thought of Niño's lice, of his inability to do anything to get rid of it, and hit her scalp harder.

She pulled her hair through a rubber band in two twists, then picked the book up off the bed, holding it with both hands. The cover had a close-up picture of a young Che, in his early twenties, sitting back and squinting at something far off in the distance. Could he see then the things he would do? How old he would look someday? She brought the picture closer to her face, so that it was only a few inches away. He didn't wear the beard yet; his skin was smooth and clear except in some rough places around his chin and upper lip. His hair looked clean. He had no wrinkles, and he wore a tie.

There was something—not exactly a knock—at her door, which scared the rooster out of his corner. He ran—claws tapping on the tile—first toward the door, and then, as if registering seconds later in his tiny brain that the noise came from just that place, away from it—flapping his wings, jerking around, running under Marielena's bed again. The rooster's frenzy had scared her more than the knock, but she immediately threw the book onto the bed, picked up the blanket, and put it back on top of the things in the box. She pushed the box under the bed with her foot, and it scraped along the floor. She heard the rooster's wing thump against the cardboard as he panicked out of its way.

She heard nothing when she put her ear to the door. She wanted to open it and see who it was, but she couldn't be sure it was a real knock, and she didn't want to call attention to herself by opening the door and seeing some neighbor—some old, bored widow, she thought, the kind the Comité recruits—across the street, sweeping her doorway.

She tiptoed back to the bed and grabbed the book—she could just open the door and start the walk to work early should any neighbors be watching from windows or porches when she checked outside. She slipped on her dusty sandals.

As she pulled open the door and stepped into the morning, she crashed into Niño, who'd been standing so close to the door that she wondered if he'd actually been leaning on it.

—Damn it, girl! he said. He held her by the shoulders, as if he'd just saved her from falling down.

—Why are . . . I thought someone was at the door. Niño, how do you know my house?

She looked past him. An older woman across the road was in her front yard beating a rug.

He smiled and his wrinkles peeked out from the corners of his eyes. He wore a straw hat and he adjusted it on his head so that she could see more of his face. The sun was behind him, making him look very dark. The light shot through the weave of the hat, turning the straw gold.

—I've seen you, he said. I don't live so far from here.

He reached a hand toward her chest, and she almost backed away, but he was only reaching for the book. He pulled it down to look at the cover.

—Excellent, Señorita, he nodded. One of my favorites. How did you know?

She was about to say, I didn't, when the rooster ran under her skirt, out between her legs, past Niño, and into the street. She gawked at the bird, her eyes big, her mouth hanging a little open. The rooster pecked at the broken pavement, looking for something to eat among the shoots of grass springing up between the cracks. He flapped his wings as he ran, lifting himself off the ground for seconds at a time. The bird squawked, as though surprised he could fly. But he was too weak to get very high, and eventually he tucked his wings close to his body, settling for the chance to run farther than he had in months. He ducked his head and darted toward the old woman's yard.

Marielena was almost crying when she started after it, but Niño put his hand up to stop her. He didn't touch her; it was a small movement meant to avoid any further attention, to keep her from trouble. But his eyes were wider than she'd ever seen them—the lines on his face hard—and she was scared because she could tell he was, too.

—You can't, he said.

Marielena looked toward the rooster. The old woman stopped beating her rug.

—Don't look at her, Niño said. She won't know which of us it belongs to. Look at me.

Marielena stared down instead at her book, her fingers like clasps on the hard cover, gripping Che's young face, the sweat from her hand leaving foggy streaks on his cheek.

—*Look* at me, Niño said again. Then he said, clenching his teeth, Please.

His hand still floated between them. It had odd brown blotches, like stains, on the palm, and was as broad as the tobacco leaves he worked with. She wished she could ignore the yellow age spots on his arms. He let the hand fall to his side.

—We should walk, he said.

When she didn't move, he said, You need to walk with me now, Señorita.

He offered her the crook of his arm, just as he had the day before. He wore an immaculately white guayabera. Marielena kept silent; she knew she smelled soap on him and swallowed hard. Nodding slowly, she turned to close her front door. It clicked shut. She turned back to him and slid her hand along the inside of his elbow, resting her fingers in a nest of coarse black arm hair.

They walked together in the direction of the factory. She thought to wave at the old woman across the street, but Niño's large frame blocked her from view. Marielena's sandals smacked the bottoms of her feet, punishing her with each step. She squeezed Niño's arm.

—Are you okay? he said.

—I don't know.

He placed his free hand on hers, curling his fingers so that he kept her holding onto him. She was surprised at how smooth his hand felt; she had thought it would be rough from the years of rolling cigars.

—You look nice for work today, he said.

She almost said, Thank you, but she remembered she was wearing the same skirt as the day before. He rubbed the back of her hand with his thumb, the soft touch almost making her forget the spoiled-looking spots on his skin. Behind them, the rooster crowed so loudly that Marielena was sure the whole street heard. She listened as the bird scrambled away, down the street in the opposite direction, followed by fast scraping noises that she recognized—a broom chasing after him. Niño squeezed her hand even tighter, and together they kept moving.

The Next Move

Two years before my wife Nilda died, she went back to Cuba against my wishes. I always said that I would never get on a plane again unless it was back to a free Cuba, which meant that in thirty-nine years of marriage, the only airplane Nilda and I had ever been on together was the flight that took us *from* Cuba, and we hadn't even sat next to each other because Celia, our daughter, perched herself between us before I could say anything. I'd always thought Nilda felt the same way as me about not going back. It was true that she hadn't seen her sisters in twenty-eight years, but I hadn't seen my *mother* in the same amount of time. I'll admit that when I got my uncle's letter saying Mamá had died, it was easier for me to be mad at my wife for wanting to return. I'll give Nilda that.

I remember taking Nilda to Miami International—Celia did not go with us because my grandson was sick (Nilda thought he was habitually underfed—I not-so-privately thought that his older sister was stealing his food, the pig). I still had that roofing job, so we were in the work van. My tools and ladders rattled with every bump in the expressway, and the traffic was so terrible that I thought God was punishing me for letting my wife go to Cuba. At home she had stuffed five hundred in cash in a sanitary napkin that she layered between two pairs of underwear. She had another three hundred she would declare, and another one hundred fifty that I shoved in her bra before we left the house so that she could offer it up as bribes, both on this side and over there. And don't remind me that it cost me over a thousand dollars for her to fly to Cuba in the first place. All this money *I* had worked to earn, and I was just handing it over to Cubans we'd always thought had picked wrong and stayed behind.

I was stuck at the Le Jeune off-ramp light. A man—back then, I would have called him a viejo—sold peanuts on one corner and another even older man (¡viejísimo!) sold churros on the other. I was hungry but refused to buy anything after handing over so much cash to my wife. So instead, while waiting for the light, I thought of sand, and gravity.

Nilda had signed us up for this mostly awful Tai Chi class at Hialeah Lakes High School. It met on Tuesday and Thursday nights and on Saturday mornings. I hated the class itself, but the ideas in it were not completely crazy, and in the van, visualizing sand sifting in and out of my foot as I pressed the brake in southwest Hialeah traffic actually calmed me. But in front of Nilda, I always pretended to hate everything about Tai Chi. I don't know why I did that. I would even make fun of her whenever I caught her doing the breathing exercises after I cut someone off with her in the van. I'd yell things like, *Breathing through your mouth won't make that comemierda a better driver*! She would never answer anyway, just put her hand on my knee and hold onto it. Her nails were always even and clean—she stopped biting them when the second grandchild had been a boy—and she still wore a bright pink polish that had looked right on her when she was young. Her knuckles had already started to swell with arthritis.

After dropping her off at the airport, I drove home while trying to make the sand do its thing and relax me. I thought about passing by Celia's first, but at the time I didn't like her husband, Ralphie, mostly because he was a grown man who liked being called *Ralphie* instead of *Raphael.* This was before they made me move in with them, before I saw how wimpy he was with his own kids, and that a man like that could only be a *Ralphie.* So instead of going north toward their neighborhood full of Monopoly houses, I headed south, through the heart of Hialeah, in the middle of rush hour, with nothing but crooked lines of cars ahead of me and not one person but me paying attention to the white dashes on the road.

A glitter-purple Buick crawled past Nilda's side of the van. The driver had the windows down, the stuff he probably called music pumping, rattling even *my* dashboard. I could hardly see the boy driving. He leaned back so far in his seat that his fingers barely reached the wheel. He picked at something on his neck, bared his teeth as he squeezed it, then inspected his fingertips when he pulled his hand away. This kid wasn't even wearing a shirt. My own grandson in his Monopoly house could grow into this kind of guy, so I said out loud, *That boy has earrings*! But without Nilda around, there was no one to make me feel better about this.

I remember trying to focus on the sand to calm down, trying to think about the string that supposedly ran through my spine and connected the top of my head to a hook or a hot air balloon or heaven—whatever ridiculous thing the Tai Chi instructor had told us to imagine—and trying not to panic, because that's when I let it sink in that Nilda would be gone an entire month.

Of course Celia called to check on me that afternoon. I hadn't even been home fifteen minutes when the phone rang, and of course she didn't ask me how *I* was feeling.

—Did Mami throw up again? Celia asked.

Nilda had been vomiting every afternoon since we decided she would go to Cuba to visit her sisters. There were five of them over there—Nilda was the oldest—and it made no sense for each of them to come over here one by one. Even I could see that. Once we finally booked the ticket, Nilda threw up every day, right around the flight's scheduled departure time. I could talk for hours about all the different things that meant, but I did nothing more about it then than bring her a glass of water to rinse out her mouth.

I told Celia, I don't know.

I was on the kitchen phone since it had the long cord, and I'd taken off my socks to clip my toenails while we talked. It needed to be done. I've always liked clipping off the nail in one whole piece, so that I can make a pile of these thick yellow half-moons on the table, which made it easier for Nilda to clean up. She always complained about it, but she never realized I was trying to make it easier for her.

I told Celia, She might have thrown up on the other side, by the gate. How would I know these things? I wasn't there.

—I'm so sorry, Papi. You know I wanted to go with you to the airport, but the baby—

My grandson was five or six then. He'd had strep throat and missed a week of kindergarten. I told Nilda that the boy getting sick was a sign from God that she shouldn't leave, but by that point, she would hear none of it. I asked Celia how he was doing.

—He's feeling better. He's *going* to school on Monday.

But she was talking to him, not to me. The second part she said louder, and away from the phone, and I heard the boy squeak, *But Mom,* and then cough.

—Come by tomorrow, Celia said. Help me with the kids, because *Carmen has been very difficult* since her brother got sick.

This, again, loud and not into the phone.

Carmen, la nieta, almost four years older than the boy. Even back then, Nilda and I could agree we had no idea what kind of girl Celia was raising, she was so heavy. I'll admit she gets that from my side, but at least I can control myself. And she was not like a girl. She never liked brushing her hair or taking a bath, and she always had some kind of syrup on her hands from all those orange ice-cream things she ate.

The boy is named Juan Carlos, and everyone but me calls him J.C., and no, neither of my grandchildren speak Spanish as well as they should. But at least they know *Abuelo,* and *Abuela.*

I promised Celia over the phone I'd come after the Saturday morning Tai Chi class.

She said, You're still going? Without Mami?

She didn't sound hurt; she was surprised. So of course I slammed the nail clippers on the table and stopped picking at the flakes on my heels. I put both feet on the ground and yelled into the phone.

—You have to go to *every* class—what do you think?—if it's gonna work! What the shit, even Mami will tell you that.

I puffed into the phone a few times to show her I was not helpless.

—What if Mami calls in the morning? Celia asked.

I was quiet for a second. Nilda's family lived in el campo—the country—so they didn't have their own phone. One of her sister's neighbors had one though, and that was the phone the whole campo would use. It was the phone Nilda's sisters used when they called from Cuba, which would cost me a fortune. They have no money to call, but for years they'd been using this system they figured out; one of them—I don't know which is which anymore, it's been so long—would call us in Miami using a collect service based in Cuba. That service cost me five dollars a minute, which is why I would have never let Nilda use it had she ever asked. When the call would come in, Nilda would refuse it, but she would call right back—the original call was just a signal that one of the sisters was at the neighbor's house. The U.S. phone company charged between ninety-five cents and a dollar twenty-eight a minute, depending on the month and the time of day. But any way you look at it, with every phone bill, Castro was ripping me off.

The two kids screamed at each other in the background, and I didn't answer Celia because I knew they were distracting her and that Ralphie was useless.

Eventually she said, Hello?

So I said, She can leave a message. I only need a message to tell me she's okay.

Celia said nothing, and I couldn't hear the kids anymore, so I said, She'll call tonight though. She said she'd walk over to the house to call. Tell me she landed okay.

Then I hung up after saying I should keep the line free.

One of the Cuban sisters put the Tai Chi idea in Nilda's head—they were always putting things in her head. After one of those expensive phone calls, Nilda brought it up. I had almost finished my rice.

Mi hermana dice—my sister says. That phrase started too many of Nilda's sentences, especially after her trip to Cuba was certain. Mi hermana dice que it's really helping with the arthritis.

Apparently, Castro required everyone over the age of fifty in Nilda's old hometown to enroll in some communist Tai Chi class—this since the USSR died and stopped helping them survive money- and medicine-wise. I couldn't help it: I imagined hundreds of people standing around in a field of dead grass, surrounded by dry palm trees, their fifty-something-year-old bodies slowly moving through ridiculous, exaggerated poses, while Castro stood up at the front, high above the crowd behind some podium, yelling some Chinese-sounding words into a bullhorn. Chinese in Spanish, what the shit, some revolution you have yourself there, Comandante, ha! Maybe someone could even get him out of those ugly madre de Dios fatigues—Karate Castro! So of course I start laughing and of course Nilda took it wrong and thought I was laughing at her. She clanged her fork against her plate.

—The way your bones crack, you shouldn't be laughing, she said.

She wiped her hands on a paper napkin as she stood up. She had eaten her whole steak, as well as all the cooked onions she'd served herself, so she only had a few grains of rice to scrape into the garbage can.

With her back to me, at the garbage can, she said, Maybe it's a good idea. Maybe he can have *one* good idea, Luis.

I'd been spinning my fork on the table, but she never turned around. I stood up and made as much noise as I could with the chair, but she still wouldn't face me. She had turned on the water, was rinsing dishes. I went up behind her and put my arms over her shoulders—she was a good eight inches shorter than me; Mamá always used to tell me the man should be taller—and she let the plate slip into the sink. I pressed her against the counter with my hips and she let her head drop forward. I remember the baby hairs on her neck.

—One? I said. Okay, this Tai Chi. Fine. But your sister hasn't eaten a whole steak like that in how long?

—Luis! she said, but she was half-laughing.

She tried to shrug off my hands, but I grabbed her harder and kissed her from behind on her neck. I felt her chest heave, her breath coming out of her mouth with no sound. It was just the two of us in that house, the only house we'd ever had in this country.

I said, Te quiero, mujer.

She lifted her head, kissed my upper arm, and said, There's flan for dessert.

Despite what I'd told Celia, I almost didn't go to Tai Chi class that morning after Nilda left because I knew people would ask me about her not being there, and I didn't know if I should tell them the truth or not, because who knows what people are loyal to anymore? And I didn't want the teacher to give me mierda. Also, Nilda hadn't called, but I'd lied and told Celia I was fine with just a message. That was the first day in decades that I didn't have café waiting for me when I woke up, and it scared me so much I got stomach cramps.

But I went, because that is what happened on Saturdays. Celia had been a student at Hialeah Lakes High, and it hadn't changed much from what I could remember, though I'd only been at the school once or twice for the Open House nights. I can tell you it looked nothing like the high schools in Cuba; this place had no windows, no courtyard, just some yellowed skylight barely lighting the main staircase of the school in what everyone called Central Plaza. Years ago, during one Open House, I asked Celia why on earth someone would build a school with no windows. She answered, *Duh,* Papi, it's a hurricane shelter. Oh, *duh,* I said back to her, trying to make fun of these English words she had started using all the time, but she didn't laugh.

The kids who roamed the halls the days me and Nilda would go to class were not at all like the kids I remembered going to school with my daughter. These were the Saturday detention kids, and by the looks of them, you probably had to try to kill a teacher to get a weekend detention. These boys—they were almost always boys, traveling in little huddles packed so tight you couldn't see who was in the middle—looked angry, their jaws clenched and outlined by thin trimmed beards. For all the time they took to get these lines on their faces straight, they couldn't manage to find clothes in the right size. I'm not stupid; I knew baggy clothes were in style—I watch enough TV to know these things—but these boys were past the point of fashion. They constantly grabbed at their crotches and I had to stop myself from saying, Come on, muchacho, we both know you don't need all that room. That day, I only saw one of those Saturday detention boys—of course he had an earring—and I almost felt sorry for him, walking all alone. By himself, he was nothing to be afraid of.

I walked into that gym without Nilda, something I hadn't done in the whole three months we'd been taking the class. The room smelled like feet—feet and sweat, and sometimes sawdust. Nilda hated when I mentioned this and would tell me to concentrate on my breathing, as if that would help. I also hated the sound people's bare feet made as they walked across the mats—a smacking sound. I don't know what these people had against socks. I never took my socks off, not once, and neither did Nilda, because we both thought that was indecent. When that foot smell hit me I breathed through my mouth like Nilda had told me to do, but I swear, when I did that, I could *taste* it.

The older women in the class standing near the back asked for Nilda. I started stretching and said, Nilda who? Then I winked at them, and they started laughing and left me alone. They found their usual spots on the mat, hiding themselves in the middle rows. The younger people in the class took up the spots in the front, near the teacher and the mirror wall. I hated the mirror wall more than the feet smell. I hated the way the girls in the class turned sideways to look at how far certain parts of them stuck out compared to others, and I hated the way the younger men in the class used the mirror to watch these girls, staring at the reflections of exposed bellies and shirts stretched tight across their chests. That mirror always made me look crooked while we practiced the warm-up Qigong moves. I *felt* straight, like my bones were aligned with the universe and everything, but all through

Crane Breathing, Cloud Hands, even during Stand Like a Pine, the mirror would show a hunched-over old man.

The instructor finally showed up, coming in from the back of the room. He wore sunglasses even though to get to the gym, you have to walk through the dark school for some time. His hair was carefully crafted into wet-looking spikes all angled forward. He had a bag slung across his chest, and he wore the same button-down shirt he wore every week, just in a different color—this week, dark blue. I hated this guy more than I hated the mirror wall, but had I ever told Nilda this she would have said I was jealous, and I don't think I could have taken that. The instructor was at least forty—still a young man, but not so young that he could get away with that hair. In retelling the tales of his own Tai Chi training, he'd made it clear that he'd been doing this a long time. His favorite phrases were *Studies have shown* and *Research has proven*, which convinced me (but of course, not Nilda) from day one that he was a fraud. Where are these studies? Who is running these comemierda tests—they don't have real jobs? At least I got Nilda to agree with me on that one—that the instructor was making these studies up—when I pointed out to her that no one would fund studying something so stupid. The instructor's name was Rodney Samuels, but he wanted us to call him Teacher, which was ridiculous because most of us in the class pronounced it something more like *tea sure.* I almost asked for my money back when I came that first day and saw that he was American. *Un Americano,* teaching this stuff? What a rip-off. I really had expected a tiny hundred-and-four-year-old Chinese man. I would have never guessed a *Rodney Samuels.*

Teacher made his way to the front, dropped the bag, and clapped twice.

—Let's get started, people, Teacher said.

Everyone was already waiting in their usual spots, so I rolled my eyes.

—Looks like we're missing someone, Teacher said. He winked at me.

—Yes, I said. I didn't know what else to say—what could I say to Rodney Samuels?—so I looked at the ground until he started talking again.

—All right then, Teacher finally said. He cracked his knuckles.

Neck, he said, turning his head all the way to the right, then all the way to the left.

The bones in my own neck cracked when I looked from side to side. I saw that the rest of the class had instinctively left a space next to me, where Nilda usually stood, so I scooted over and took up the extra space, which, when you saw it in the stupid mirror, made me look separated from everyone.

—Shoulders, Teacher said.

We worked our way down, pushing all the negative energy out through our feet. Honestly, I never felt this—like something was getting pushed out—but I *could* feel it moving down, and I did feel more relaxed thanks to the sand concept. I could pace myself with this idea—that the sand sifted down, filling my legs—and sometimes I even let myself imagine that the sand was from all the shores I'd ever known, and that Nilda had that same special sand falling in her, filling her feet.

—Send energy to the kidneys, Teacher said.

This meant to rub our lower backs, but of course this guy was a super professional Tai Chi Grand Master Flash something or other, so he had to say things like a hippie. I didn't move and he finally just glared at me and said, Rub your kidneys, Luis.

After we beamed what Teacher felt was the right amount of energy from our brains to our kidneys, Teacher said, Ready position, and everyone shifted so that their feet were parallel and shoulder-width apart.

We slowly moved from that into the Bow and Arrow stance, which made everyone squat a little. Teacher began his routine chanting.

—Breath, focus on breath. Exhale. Inhale. Counting, flowing. Energy. Thought. Focus.

Teacher's voice tried to be soothing—the words came out far apart—but to me he sounded ridiculous.

I have not mentioned how silly everyone looked doing this—maybe because many of us older people were on the heavy side—so I usually closed my eyes to help me not laugh. But that day, I had to close them to stop staring at the space in the mirror where I normally saw Nilda. She always looked the silliest of all—because she tried so hard to believe all this Tai Chi magic—holding, in front of her belly, an energy ball full of nothing. Her shoulders rose and fell when she breathed, and she was good at concentrating, hardly looking at me. But I watched her, looking so silly, thinking, *How did we ever get here*?

Teacher kept chanting, Focus. Expand. Contract. Focus.

I don't know how I was supposed to focus with all of his flower talk, and with Nilda so far away. It's not that I thought she wouldn't come back—who defects in *that* direction?—but that she needed to go back so badly, with or without me.

My jaw ached and the bones in my hands felt locked. I wanted to run out of the class and go sit in my van. When I opened my eyes, Teacher was staring at me like I had said something out loud. He nodded and said, Let go of the thoughts that come to your mind. If thoughts come to your mind, let them go. Energy follows thought.

I tried to let go of the infuriating way Teacher tried to sound old and wise by saying things like he was in a *Star Wars* movie. I hated that. But I nodded and closed my eyes again. But you tell me how to let go of how useless you look, standing there with your empty energy ball and your warped reflection and your missing wife.

Of course the sand kept shifting. I moved from Ward Off Right to Ward Off Left—my two favorite positions—the only thing I'd practice at home while Nilda busied herself in the kitchen and couldn't see me. At certain points in these stances, my arms were in the air, palms flat, ready to chop at anything that might attack me. Teacher saved these for close to the end of our session, and by then I almost felt strong. But when I moved from right position to left position, I saw nothing there. I mean, I had never *seen* anything but Nilda, her back to me, with her hands in front of her, ready to fight that same imaginary attacker I would fight.

Teacher ended class by giving another one of what he called his lectures. Teacher felt it was critical to relate stories about the development of Tai Chi over the ages to convince us of Tai Chi's health benefits. He quoted absurd statistics: that ninety-eight percent of miscarriages are caused by the mother's poor posture; that ninety-five percent of strokes *and* heart attacks are caused by poor breathing techniques; that seventy-three percent of people who do Tai Chi live to be over a hundred.

Teacher made us sit around like children at story hour. I sat down on the mat and rubbed my knees. Teacher sat in front of the group in a red plastic chair.

He said, One day, this guy named Yang Lee was walking through a forest. He had just come down from a mountain, this real famous mountain, after studying for many years. He was studying all sorts of things, mind and body things, martial arts and whatnot.

Teacher licked his lips like a lizard, his tongue darting all the way out instead of just pulling in his lips like a decent man. He did this constantly. I thought this was disgusting, and had said so to Nilda. She'd only said, Why do you notice these things? The lizard lip-licking punctuated Teacher's sentences. I thought I'd pull all my hair out before he finished.

—So Yang Lee's walking, and he sees this snake, right? And this snake's fighting with this crane, right? So Yang Lee gets this crazy idea. He realizes, the way they fight, they use the other's movement to fight back.

Teacher reclined in the chair like he was done, and I hoped to God he was, because I understood. Other people looked around, confused. The two old ladies who were friends with each other shrugged their shoulders. One girl kept braiding her bangs. But *I* knew what he was saying, and I wanted him to shut up. I swear all his energy felt focused right at me.

—Guys, Teacher said, The snake and the crane, they were using the energy from the other to go into the next move.

When I think about that story now, I worry that maybe I killed Nilda, being who I was—how I was—with her. That I stole from her our whole life without giving her enough for any more moves. But that day in class, when Teacher said what he said, I thought about it the other way around. Nilda was somewhere she'd fought me to be. I stared at my socks, at the gray spots on the bottoms marking my toes and heels, places where the cotton was thin and useless. Only the leftover sand in my legs kept me from flying out of that gym.

Teacher said, This was Yang Lee's discovery. We now call this life energy, or Chi.

I heard some people say, Oooh, and I reminded myself that you had to be half-stupid to believe what someone named Rodney Samuels had to say about someone named Yang Lee.

When I got to Celia's house, Ralphie's truck was hunkered in their driveway—he was not the kind of man who worked on Saturdays. I parked behind him, sitting in my van for a minute to prepare for their animal children.

Celia stood in the kitchen making chicken soup for lunch. Half of a raw chicken sat on the cutting board. Celia was chopping carrots and throwing them into the pot. She asked me if Nilda had called.

I said, You add the carrots at the end. What's wrong with you?

Nilda was a much better cook, and though she'd tried to teach Celia these things, our daughter bought cookbooks in English. Celia leaned over to kiss me on the cheek.

—I'm trying it different this time, she said. What about Mami?

—I don't know, I said. Why are you doing that with the carrots?

I grabbed a spoon and started to fling carrots out of the pot, into the sink, to rescue them.

—Papi, stop! she said, her hands scrambling for the slippery chunks. J.C. likes the pieces soggier anyways.

She grabbed the spoon from me with one hand and tossed the carrots back in the soup with the other. She wiped her hand on my sleeve, pushing me from the pot, and said, J.C. is in his room if you want to see him. I told him Abuelo was coming today.

I turned to leave and said, I don't want any of that soup—it's gonna taste too much like carrots.

Juan Carlos was sitting up in bed watching cartoons. The bed was draped in the astronaut sheets that he'd picked out himself, and his hair was flattened on one side from leaning on his pillow. He didn't have a shirt on, and I could see the boy's ribs. I thought, *No wonder he's sick.*

—Muchacho, I said.

Juan Carlos turned from the TV and said, Abuelo! He raised his arms for a hug, but then started coughing. It sounded wet, and the boy had not been taught to cover his mouth. I stood in the doorway, but the coughing didn't stop, so I came over, sat on the bed, and smacked him on the back a few times.

—Okay, okay, I said. I get it, you're sick.

I couldn't help it though; I pulled him to me, kissed him on his sweaty hair.

—It hurts when I talk, he whispered, pointing to his throat.

I grabbed his shoulders and held the boy away from myself, pretending to inspect him. He doesn't look like his father or his mother.

—Don't talk then, I said.

The boy frowned.

—I'm hungry, he said.

—Really! That's a good sign. Means you're getting better.

—Nuh-uh, he said.

He buried his head into my side. I turned off the TV with the remote.

—I'm going to tell you a story to make you better, okay? Then you'll eat soup.

Juan Carlos nodded into my armpit. I looked out the window, through the chain-link fence, at the neighboring yard. A little girl I had never seen outside before played on a swing—the same swing set model Ralphie and Celia had bought. She was alone and so young that she did not have on a shirt, only shorts. When Celia was small, she ran around the same way, until she was old enough to know she should put one on. As a child, I didn't wear a shirt in Cuba until the day I started school.

—Okay, I said. When I was a boy like you—you're five, right?

Juan Carlos pushed off of me with two balled-up fists. He nodded, his forehead wrinkled with angry lines.

—I'm kidding, I know you're five, come on.

He crashed back into my side and looked out the window, too.

—When I was five like you, I used to play outside, but not like those kids, not on swings. We didn't have things like that there, we had better things outside, en el campo—the country, you know? Did you know your abuelo was a country boy?

He shook his head no, but I'm sure I had told him before. We watched the girl swing for what felt like a long while. When me and Nilda came from Cuba, before we had the house, we shared a duplex in Liberty City with my brother—they'd come over two months before us—and it didn't have a real backyard, just some poured concrete, a little slab. It was fenced in on all sides, so that you couldn't see your neighbor's concrete slab. Nights I worried—sometimes out loud to Nilda—that Celia somehow wouldn't *grow* right, from playing back there. It was not safe to play in the front yard, and she was always tearing up her knees on the slab. Nilda would say, *You made the right choice in bringing us here,* to have faith, but then she would turn her back to me in her sleep.

—What are you *doing*? Carmen said from the door.

Carmen leaned against the doorframe, arms crossed over her rolls of stomach. Her cheeks were very red and she was sweaty. Her legs had dirt smudges on them, and her hair was pulled back in a failure of a ponytail, with frizzy pieces loose and sticking to the sides of her face. When I said, Carmen! she ran in the room and threw her arms around me, pushing herself onto the bed, on me, and almost squashing Juan Carlos in the process.

While the boy coughed, she said, Abuelo, I was outside and there was a grasshopper and I tried to grab it but it jumped through the fence and I couldn't get it.

—Madre de Dios, chica! Did you wash your hands at least? Where's your mother?

I tried to look past her to the kitchen, but you have to understand, it's like these kids run the place. Carmen thrust her arm out to point at the TV screen. There was a line of dirt wedged in the bend of her elbow.

She said, Why is the TV off? We were watching it.

This is how she talks to her abuelo.

I said, How are you watching TV if you are outside? You were playing while Juan Carlos is stuck in here, sick?

—J.C. doesn't care. Right?

Juan Carlos shrugged. I rubbed my knee.

—I'm telling your brother a story, I said. Sit down, I'll tell you both.

—Mom's making soup, Carmen said.

—Sit. I pointed to the farthest edge of the bed, but Carmen planted herself on the floor and cupped her knees in her hands.

—Okay. So when I was a little boy, I used to—

—How old were you? Carmen said.

—I said that already, before you came in. I was five, like Juan Carlos.

Carmen cocked her head and leaned forward. She said, I *know* J.C. is five.

—I was five and this was in Cuba, so when we used to play outside, we didn't have swing sets like that little girl out there or like you two. I rode horses, and I played in the river, and we made a swing with a tire and a rope.

—You didn't have *horses*, Carmen said.

Juan Carlos looked up at me to see which one of us was telling the truth.

I said, What the hell? What do you know about anything?

I threw up my hands, but she knew I wouldn't hit her.

—Mom says Cuba is just like Miami, she said. And there are *no* horses *here*.

I didn't even know where to start explaining how wrong she was—how there *were* horses in Miami, just not around where *they* lived. There were horses north of the city, in Broward County, and way down south, where some of the Cuban fruit vendors still living there kept old horses on small patches of land. And of course, Miami is nothing like Cuba.

—Listen, muchacha, I said. I was trying to be patient, really. I said, Your mother is wrong *a lot*. Let me tell you something about caballos—

—That's horses, right? she said. Or is it onions?

She stretched herself out and rolled around on the floor as she said this, her hair tangling around her head and getting in her mouth. Even now the teachers say she has problems in school with her attention—her parents give her *medicine* for this.

—But how can you play in a river if it's moving? Juan Carlos said. He rubbed his throat.

—Onions is *cebollas*, not caballos! Madre de Dios! What's wrong with you? I said.

—Yeah, *Abuelo*, you can only play in *pools*, Carmen said, nodding at Juan Carlos.

—Is Abuela in this story? the boy said.

I looked at him, opened my mouth to talk, and couldn't say anything.

Carmen rearranged herself on the floor so that she was on her stomach, her chin in her hand.

—Do you *really* remember being five? she said, scratching her head.

I stood up from the bed and said, Can't I just tell a goddamn story!

I stepped over her to leave the room—almost fell from taking too wide a step—and caught myself on the doorframe. Finally I heard Celia say, Papi? She came into the living room with a wooden spoon in her hand. Carmen squeezed past me, pushing my waist out of her way, and stood between me and my daughter.

—Abuelo said "goddamn," she said. I only said it *now* 'cause Abuelo said it *before*, so I can't get in trouble for saying it *now*.

I walked past Carmen and Celia, out through the kitchen, to the side door where I came in. I didn't look at either of them. I couldn't help but look at that miserable, half-prepared soup on my way through the kitchen.

—Papi, what happened? Celia said.

I had my hand on the doorknob. My daughter stood staring at me, confused, with a knife in one hand and *another* carrot in the other. Madre de Dios, she was determined to ruin that soup.

I didn't think about what I said next. I yelled, You can't even talk to those shitty kids!

I could hear Celia punishing Carmen from the driveway, and I knew by the time I made it to the van that my words would find Nilda, even a month from then, and that I would hear it from her, because I got in trouble even when I told the truth.

The answering machine light was not blinking when I got home. I didn't know what else to do, so I sat down in my recliner and turned on the television, flipped to the Spanish-language news, and waited for the phone to ring. I knew Nilda well enough to be sure she wouldn't just *forget* to call. Her not calling meant that something else—her sisters, a tour of her old house, the whole damn island—was more important than me.

A report came on about a shooting at a nearby restaurant, but I stopped paying attention once I found out it wasn't one we'd ever been to. I smoothed over my eyelids with my fingertips and then pressed my fingers to the bridge of my nose, thinking Nilda might never call me.

The weather report came on and showed a Cuba covered with thick green, yellow, and orange radar bands. Heavy rains had been drenching the area since Friday afternoon, and for a second I worried that Nilda's plane had never even taken off, and that she had spent the night sleeping on an airport floor. But she would have definitely known to call me from there. I even started to laugh. I said to the TV, Madre de Dios. Look at that storm. What am I thinking?

I didn't know what to do for lunch now that I'd left Celia's. I didn't know what to do for dinner, either. Meals were something I couldn't remember ever worrying about, and I already started feeling how unfair to me it was that I had to start worrying then. Nilda had always made something light on Saturdays for lunch—she was worried about our Chi. She'd make salad, with avocados, and I would complain that I was still hungry—I'd call our lunch rabbit food—but I never really meant it. Nilda had to know that.

The phone rang while I sat there, pinching my eyes in the recliner. I almost cried, Gracias a Dios—Thank you, God!—for listening!—when I picked up.

On the line I heard Carmen say, Abuelo?

—Why are you calling? I said. Your grandma might—

—Mom said I had to call to say sorry for before.

I clutched the receiver to my face. I had to lean against the kitchen wall. Maybe I had stood up too fast—I thought I was having a heart attack. In the background on the phone, Celia said, I told you not to tell him I made you, malcriada! You don't listen? What kind of an apology is that? Then the boy coughing, saying, Carmen, lemme talk to Abuelo.

I should have hung up to keep the line free, but I could barely make out the boy's voice behind Celia's, who yelled, You're gonna hurt your throat and you have to go to school on Monday.

In the quiet that followed, Juan Carlos said, Carmen, please, he didn't finish the story.

When I sat down on the kitchen floor, a piece of toenail jammed into my palm. I stared at it lodged there, shocked I'd let one fall from the pile.

—Mom said to *shut up*, J.C., Carmen said. I heard Juan Carlos start to cry, and then cough, and then cry some more. I heard Celia try to calm him down, but the boy wailed.

I wanted to say, Don't cry, muchacho. Crying is for girls—you know that. But to say it would have made me a liar, because I was crying, too—because of the toenail, and because I didn't want to finish the story for Juan Carlos. Crying harder when I thought of Nilda walking a mile through all that rain just to get a busy signal, or an answering machine. It might be days before she tried again.

I heard the girl say, Goddamn, and then her mother yelling something at her. Then the girl screamed, But *Abuelo* said it! After a click, I heard the dial tone. I hung up on my end and sat there on the tile, along with my toenails and all the other things Nilda had always swept up for the both of us, and waited for another call.

Nilda finally called that night. Of course she called. Called me once a week the whole time she was gone. I always accepted the charges rather than use her callback system, because the cost didn't matter—she never wanted to speak for very long.

Her last week there, she asked me if I thought she should stay another month. I said she should do what she wanted, but that if she was really asking me, then no, I wanted her to come home. I told her Celia needed her, I needed her—almost told her about the snake and the crane, but the call was costing enough as it was—and that all her sisters had each other, so she was needed more here. What was left for her there to do? She said, of course, of course. I didn't think about what I'd said until I saw her sinking down the airport terminal toward me, her face red from crying so many goodbyes, her hands empty. She had left everything there, even her suitcases, for her sisters to have, everything except her driver's license and her plane ticket.

It was, for a while, the same as before she left. She told me about her old farm and how her sisters managed, how things were not as bad as we liked to think they were, though I made her admit they were still bad. She told me how her old school was still a school, how she had sat in her old desk once the students were gone for the day, and how she had hardly fit in it. We slept in the same bed and she said she missed me, and in the darkness of our bedroom I said I missed her, too. I even told her about the sand in us both, how Tai Chi was miserable without her—more miserable than usual. But she didn't ask anything about the class. She kept talking. She told me how she had taken a day and gone back to where *I'd* lived, riding a bus to get there—a two-hour trip, longer than the plane ride to Cuba from Miami—to see my old house and the church where we got married, which she told me was not there anymore. I hid my eyes under my hand. After breathing for a minute, I asked her what was there instead.

—Nothing, she said, pulling the sheet up around her. The walls are there, but it's empty.

She fell asleep before I could think of the right thing to say.

After missing almost a month of classes, we lost our spot in Tai Chi, and Nilda never bothered to sign us back up again. Which was fine with me, I told her, because me and *Rodney Samuels* were not on good terms. From her spot by the sink, my dirty plate in her hand, she only grunted. So I stayed at the table.

Even weeks after coming back, Nilda kept telling Celia the same stories from her trip, but Celia could not remember any of the faces that went with the names Nilda mentioned, and Nilda grew frantic trying to jog her memory. *But they are your tías,* she would say. For her part, Celia tried to remember, but the kids got bored and asked to leave the table. Of course Ralphie said no, and in moments like that one, the man has some sense. But I understand why they don't want to listen. Because for me, Cuba the *place* has been a story ever since Nilda came back. She came back and told it to me, and now it is worse than nothing.

After a few months, after we found out she had the heart thing that eventually led to the stroke, Nilda started talking about being buried in Cuba, which I thought was impossible, and which I also thought was a stupid idea because she'd lived here longer than there. And we'd already bought plots in the Miami Gardens Cemetery—we'd even paid them off by then. In the end, she stopped talking about it, stopped talking about how sad it would be that her sisters might never see her grave. When God finally took her, I put her in the Miami ground with the promise that someday soon I'd rest next to her. But there have been too many years since then with me still moving, and I don't know what I did to deserve that. My mother did it right: she died less than a year after she lost my father. When my uncle wrote from Cuba with the news, he said that my parents were like caged finches. When one finch dies, the other finch gets sick soon after. When one dies, you can kiss the other goodbye, and that's how it should be. That's how my uncle wrote it, but of course, he wrote it in Spanish. And of course, in Spanish, it sounds much sweeter.

Animal Control

Danny shifted the phone to his other ear and restated the question, this time using a tone the policeman would not object to.

—I would just like to know, Sir, he said, What exactly I'm supposed to do, Sir, with Eddie's ferret.

He paced around the room, stepping over a box of Eddie's things, which his mother and sister had packed up the day before while picking out the suit for Eddie to be buried in. The ferret, across the room and in its cage, clung to the wire mesh with its nails, awaiting the pronouncement of its fate. Its water dish was empty, and it balanced on its back legs, standing upright inside the plastic bowl. Danny thought it looked like the thing was getting its graying fur ready for a bath. The ferret was officially his problem: when Eddie's mother had come for the suit, she said, in Spanish, that she would not be taking *that rat*.

—It isn't our concern, Mr. Cabrera. We told you that yesterday when you called?

—But I don't even *like* this ferret. It's not my ferret.

On behalf of the entire Miami-Dade County police force, the officer again apologized for Danny's loss.

—Listen, Danny said. Eddie was my roommate, not my friend, not my gay boyfriend or whatever, so you can forget that shit about my loss, unless you mean the extra $700 in rent I gotta come up with now.

The police officer was quiet. The ferret began chewing on the cage, jerking the wires back and forth with its teeth—something it had done nonstop the night before, when Eddie never came home.

—My point, Mr. Cabrera? the officer finally said, Is that the ferret is not the department's concern. I can give you the number to an animal shelter if you want to surrender it? Otherwise, I'm going to have to ask you to stop calling us about this issue.

Danny wrote down the number. He made the officer repeat it three times before hanging up.

He needed to get rid of the ferret before their landlady could show the place to a new roommate. The landlady didn't allow pets, so Danny's dog still lived with his parents, but Eddie had gotten permission to keep the ferret by going over Danny's head and talking to the landlady himself. She'd never even seen a ferret, and he'd managed to convince her that it was only a little more alive than a hamster.

The landlady had called after seeing the news about the shooting on TV. Danny hadn't been home, but the message she left on the machine was long enough to suggest she hadn't noticed: It's not *my* Eddie they are talking about, no? Because the shooting was at the Chili's allí mismo. But neither of you have guns, so it has to be some *other* Eddie, no? Sorry to be una vieja metida, but I just *had* to call and make sure. Bueno, for the love of God, be careful out there. This Miami es una locura.

Eddie *did* have a gun—he'd told Danny that—but Danny had never seen it. Eddie had felt compelled, for safety reasons, to tell

Danny about the gun, emphasizing that it was registered and legal.

—You're not living with some thug, Eddie told him three months before, just after he'd moved in.

—I don't care if you are or not, Danny said back from his spot on the sofa. Just keep your shit in your room and your piss in the toilet.

According to the police report, Eddie had fired one shot before being hit himself. The other guy did a better job, getting him right in the heart, and Eddie was dead before the ambulance got there. The other guy died a few hours later, at the hospital. Witnesses gave drastically different accounts, but most agreed that the fight had started over either a parking spot or a spot on the waitlist at Chili's. Thursday nights were always busy at that Chili's, and a lot of car clubs used the parking lot to show off their rides. Danny had only been to that Chili's once: after finding a hair in one of the mozzarella sticks, he'd never gone back. That's what he told the woman from the *Miami Herald* when she contacted him for a comment. The reporter asked, annoyed, Weren't you guys *friends*? He had a hard time hearing her over the ferret's crazed cage gnawing. He went to tell it to shut up and realized he didn't even know the ferret's name.

The woman at the shelter's front desk slid a clipboard and pen across to him.

—The ferret's in the car, he explained when she looked around and behind him, then *at* him like he was crazy.

—Shouldn't you go get it? It's like, a hundred degrees outside.

—We used to keep it outside, he lied. It'll deal.

The woman raised her eyebrows and turned away toward her computer, her fingers running across the keyboard to type something. Danny found a seat in the row of chairs farthest from her and her desk.

The form tucked into the clipboard read *Miami-Dade Animal Control* in big letters across the top. It asked for the animal's name, type, and age. It asked how long it had been owned. It asked for the date of its last veterinary exam, for a list of the shots it had received, for information regarding its temperament (good with kids? good with other pets?), and for the reason for surrender. This last question was the only one that Danny could answer easily. *Owner dead,* he wrote, feeling that answer justified all the blanks he'd left on the form.

He looked up from the clipboard. Across from him, a white man in a volunteer T-shirt was helping a very old person fill out the form, translating the questions into broken Creole. At their feet lay a very tired looking mutt, bigheaded and silver around the muzzle, panting. The dog spread its legs out behind it, getting as much of the cold tile floor in contact with its belly as it could, and Danny thought of the trick he'd taught his own dog—Go long!—where the dog did the same thing but on command. The translator was having trouble explaining something to the old man. When he noticed Danny staring at them, he said, Do you speak Creole?

Danny shook his head no.

—This poor guy, the volunteer said, Has had this dog for nine years. The cops come around his place, see the dog in the yard, and decide the thing is part pit bull, and so he has to get rid of him. Turns out the dog's unregistered, too, and this guy thinks that's the problem, so he's here to fix that. But pit bulls—even mixes—are illegal in this county. I can't seem to get across to him that he can't register the dog. The form he's filling out is to relinquish the damn thing. I'm trying to explain to him that they're going to put the dog down.

The dog looked up at the man doing the talking, then put its head back on the floor. The dog's owner rested his flip-flop clad foot on the dog's back, nestling his heel in the dog's graying fur. The dog reached its head around and started licking the man's dusty toes.

—I'm trying to get rid of this ferret, Danny said.

He didn't know what else to say; he'd already told the guy he didn't speak Creole.

The man nodded and turned back to the dog's owner, who was now bent over, speaking very softly and stroking the dog's broad head. The old man's hands had big knobby knuckles, and the skin was dry and ashy around his flat, pink fingernails. The dog closed its eyes and Danny swore he saw the corners of the dog's mouth twitch in a smile. The old man bent down even closer to his pet and whispered, Nou se zanmi. He sat up and said it again, louder, to the man translating. Then, without the translator's help, the old man put his skinny hand over his heart, looked right at Danny, and said, *We are friends.* He moved his hand from his heart back to his dog and scratched the animal in long passes down its sides. The dog rolled over and surrendered its belly. Danny could smell it then, dirt and fur and something damp. The old man kept scratching and said, *You know friends? Understand?*

Danny jumped out of the chair, throwing the clipboard on the empty seat next to him. The dog jerked its head toward him, suddenly very alert.

—I barely fucking knew the guy, alright? he said to the old man.

He charged out from the room, ignoring the gush of panicked Creole and the translator's shushes. He headed to his car, his hands shaking as he fumbled for the keys in his pocket. As he came out from under the shade of the shelter's entrance, the sun blared down on him, making it hard to see where he was going, and he crashed into a lady who was bringing in a box full of cats. He said, Oh shit, then, Excuse me, and he even held the door open for her, but she didn't say excuse me back. She just glared at him over her box of cats, their tails swishing above the cardboard like ghosts, and made a point not to say thank you as she went through the door.

The ferret was dead by the time he unlocked the car. It looked damp inside its carrier, like it had been sweating, though he didn't know if ferrets could sweat. He'd only been inside for five minutes—the thing couldn't survive five minutes in the car? Jesus Christ! he said out loud.

He got in the driver's seat and started the car, opening the carrier and pulling the ferret out as he backed up. It felt somehow slimy in his hand, wet without being wet. Danny dropped it back in the carrier and refused to give in to his weird, sudden desire to sniff it, to know exactly what a recent death smelled like. The last time he saw Eddie was the afternoon of the shooting, when he walked into the bathroom while Eddie stood in front of the mirror, dousing himself with cologne. Eddie had left the door open, a small sign he was growing comfortable in the apartment, a sign Danny would not think about until the *Miami Herald* reporter's question. The cologne was musky, earthy—almost suffocating—and it surrounded Eddie like a mist. Danny watched the cloud sink and settle on Eddie's shoulders. Then Eddie turned to him and sprayed him square in the chest, leaving a wet circle right over his heart, and they laughed together at this, their first and last joke.

Danny forced himself into traffic and two blocks later, pulled into a fast food drive thru, ordering nothing but a large glass of ice water. The voice in the speaker even said, *Water*? That's *it*?

After grabbing the waxy paper cup, he swerved into a parking spot, ripped off the plastic lid, and dunked the ferret's head into the water. Pieces of ice clinked against other pieces of ice, but the ferret made no noise. He pulled it out and shook it a little. Soaked like that, it looked even more dead, and Danny tried harder not to cry. He dunked the ferret in the water over and over again, yelling, Oh come on! Come *on*! each time. The ferret grew stiff. It stared at him and said nothing. But Danny kept dunking, kept listening for a squeak or a scratch, giving up only after the last piece of ice had melted, only after he couldn't ignore that he felt nothing, that his fingers had gone numb.

Noche Buena

While my dad changed the oil in his brand new '96 Chevy Tahoe, I asked him if I could ride out to the Christmas Eve party—or like he calls it, *El Venticuatro*—in my own car. This year, the holiday would take over my Tía Eva's house, and I wanted to show off the car to my cousins. All of them had gotten stuck with handed-down Mom Rides. But since our Toyota had gone to my big sister, Teresa, I'd been the first cousin ever who had a say in what car they got. So I drove a barely used bright blue Integra, dropped low, with dark tints and chrome spider rims, mostly all paid for by my own part-time job at Discount Auto Supply but also partly an early Christmas present from my dad. I asked for permission while he was under the truck, his back against the driveway. I thought maybe he'd be distracted enough to say yes by accident.

—Why? Papi said. Are you taking a girl?

His voice came from underneath the engine. I could only see his legs in their work pants sticking out like he'd been run over.

I rolled my eyes because he couldn't see me and said, No, Papi.

—Do you have some children I don't know about that you have to take?

He slid out from underneath the truck and stood up. His beige T-shirt had no oil on it, but smudges covered his hands and wrists. He kept them far from his T-shirt. He shifted his weight, leaned on the truck's grill, and pretended to want a real answer.

—No, Papi, I don't got any kids.

Oil stained the driveway, two round spots by his feet. Neither looked fresh.

After a second, he stood up straight and pushed at his glasses with the back of his wrist, but he still got a little grease on the bottom of the frames.

—Then I don't see why you need to take your car, if there's no family *you* have to take.

He turned around and wiped the bumper with a rag. The Tahoe was about the only thing he'd ever owned and owed nothing on. He paid for it in cash, from his smaller roofing jobs—neighbors' houses, tool sheds. Some of that cash went to the down payment of my Integra, but I planned on paying him back as soon as I got more hours at work.

—Besides, he said, still wiping, We are all going to your tía's house together.

—Almost all, I said, to piss him off.

It worked, because he kept wiping even though the bumper shined, and he paid attention to some spot that wasn't even there.

He said, Go inside and tell Mami to bring me some café and a glass of water.

I kept standing there, even when he walked away toward the garage. I didn't notice I'd been holding my breath until I closed the front door behind me and yelled out what he wanted to my mom.

This was the first year we'd be taking the Tahoe to Noche Buena, and I knew it was a big deal for Papi—he washed and waxed the truck every Sunday the way other people go to church—but it was a big deal when *anyone* in my family got a new ride. Some years, Noche Buena turned into a South Miami Auto Show. Back when Tía Yola got her Caddy—I must have been eight or nine because Abuelo was alive and still working with my dad—she had rolled up the driveway, honking nonstop. All of us ran out from the backyard to see who it was. And there was Tía, and two of my cousins, Braulio y Mirta, in the backseat, sitting in this cream-colored tank. That Caddy was so bright I had to squint and shade my eyes with my hand. It was just a standard edition, not pimped out—no rims, no CD changer, *nothing*—but the way we all stood around it, you'd think Jesus was in the driver's seat. We piled in seven at a time and rode around the block like a one car parade. I got to sit up in the front on my mom's lap, and Tere was sent to the backseat—she was known to have a thing for car horns. Every time we'd pass the house we'd wave at the cousins and tíos still waiting for their turn and they'd wave back to the boat full of Cuban refugees. That Cadillac was the only thing us kids could talk about all afternoon and night, until Fake Santa would show up around midnight. It was all about who got what presents and guessing which tío they'd suckered into wearing that hundred-year-old Santa costume after that.

This was also going to be the first year that the five of us probably wouldn't show up together. Teresa schemed on coming later with her boyfriend, Ruben, who I guess was actually her fiancé now that he'd given her a ring. They'd been going out for three years—I'd been calling him Ruby for at least two—but still, Papi had never let him come to Noche Buena before, saying he just wasn't part of the family. He hadn't been allowed to meet all the extended people until things were serious between them, and *serious* in my family means prometida with a ring to prove it.

Papi never figured that Tere would even try to miss our family's Noche Buena to go to Ruben's instead—that's just not done—so when my mom warned him two nights before that Tere planned to ask him for permission, he started planning in his head all the reasons why the answer was No. He rehearsed them that night with my mom at dinner, when it was just the four of us, since Tere was at her night class at Miami-Dade.

—She's been going to our Noche Buena for twenty years, Papi said, cutting up his chicken. I don't see why that has to change now.

He had no shirt on because he'd come late from work. He'd been too hungry to shower and change before eating, so the dirty shirt got thrown over the back of the couch as he'd stomped in.

—Manuel, Mami said to him, She wants to come, but she wants to spend some time with his family, too. I think we have to compromise with her, Papi.

My mom scooped rice onto my little sister's plate, more than she'd be able to eat. Gisela sat swinging her legs under the table, trying to kick me.

—She has to do what I say, Papi said.

—Of course she does, I'm not saying she doesn't.

Mami finished serving Gisela and then started filling my plate with rice and chicken. When my dad's pissed, it's like no one's at the table except him, his food, and maybe my mom. We just watch him chew.

Mami said, Last year you told Tere that when things were more serious with Ruben, you would think about Noche Buena.

—You can't get more serious than engaged, I said, pushing my rice around.

My dad let his fork hit his plate but he didn't look at me. Like always, my mom kept talking to keep him calm.

—Ruben's family has invited her the past three years. They even asked us to come.

—I ain't going to that shit, I said. Gisela's foot finally hit my knee. I bit down on my bottom lip and looked at her until she looked away. She'd had to almost slide under the table to reach my leg, and she stayed there now to hide from me.

—Ya, Manny. No one is talking to you, Mami said. Sit up, Gisela.

Papi just kept eating—got the food into his mouth fast, packed it in, like the rice could move from his mouth into his ears and plug them up, so he wouldn't have to listen to what Mami said. After dinner, Gisela took the dishes from the table to the sink, and Mami brought out a plate with the postre—guayaba and cream cheese on Cuban crackers, Papi's favorite. Mami had already put the cream cheese on the crackers for him.

When she brought over the plate, I could smell the perfume of the soap she's used for at least as long as I've been alive—a smell like lemons and baby powder that announced to the world *Smell me, I'm clean.*

—Things are different now that she has that ring, Mami told him. She let her hand fall from the back of his head to his bare shoulder.

My sister would be Mrs. Ruben Gutierrez in less than a year, and her new husband would be the first guy in our family to have ever gone to college. Ruben was at Florida International getting a degree in business or business management or something with business. So when Papi would come home from work smelling like burned paper, with tar on his pants, and if Ruben was over, he would ask him, *How's business? Business okay*? and he'd laugh and pretend to choke on the smell of Ruben's cologne, and Tere would get all mad.

Cracker crumbs floated in Papi's dark goatee.

—I want her at Eva's house by seven, he said while Mami rinsed dishes in the sink, Even if she has to miss the dinner at that boy's house. She eats with us at seven.

I grabbed a cracker and a chunk of the guayaba off his plate, but he didn't say anything. I could hear him chewing hard. Mami came over and put her wet hand on his. The chain of bubbles from the dish soap slid off her hand and disappeared into a spot on the tablecloth.

Papi didn't move, but he kept chewing. Mami smiled at me. Her hair was pulled back, but pieces sprung out around her head like her shadow was about to jump her. I smiled back, proud I'd asked Papi about driving the Integra myself, rather than going through Mami like we always did, because she looked so tired just then.

On the morning of Noche Buena, I woke up and went to the kitchen, where Mami was cooking congrí and frying croquetas even though my tía had told her not to bring anything. Gisela was picking out clothes and taking outfits, still on the hanger, to the kitchen to show my mom. She'd just turned ten, and so she took how she'd look at Noche Buena serious because she still made out with a lot of presents. Teresa had woken up early to blow out her hair and put big rollers in it so it would look straight. Mami stood behind Tere, with a thick chunk of my sister's hair in her hand and fifty pins in her mouth. She twisted Tere's hair around Velcro rollers, big as spaghetti sauce jars.

—Mami, come on. You're gonna get hair in the rice! I told her.

—Cállate, Manny, said Tere, not moving her head.

—*You* shut up, I told her.

—Ya, Mami said, drawing out the A. She held the pins between her teeth.

—I'm just sayin', I said, opening the fridge.

—Manny, please take a shower, Mami said. And make sure you shave. I don't want anyone saying you look dirty. And don't forget to take your senior class pictures to give to people tonight. I have too much to worry about. *You* don't forget.

She sounded like a pirate in the movies because of how she couldn't move her teeth.

—Alright, alright. Calm down, I said. Where's Papi?

—He went to your work to get stuff to clean the tires of the truck. I don't know why he always has to wait until the last minute to do everything. I told him we had to be at Tía Eva's by two. It's twelve-thirty and he's cleaning tires!

Gisela brought in a thin purple dress and Mami shook her head No.

Then Tere made a sucking sound through her teeth because Mami had pulled too hard on her hair. Her head jerked forward in a reflex and one of her long fingernails scratched at the tugged-on spot. Tere's eyes even watered.

Mami said, Ay Dios mío, Teresita, this wouldn't hurt so much if you would just stay put.

I showered and shaved like Mami told me to, but kept a goatee, which she said was fine because it didn't look raggedy now that the lines between the mustache and chin had grown in. Eighteen years and lots of frijoles to get those to grow, she said. She had Gisela wearing a red velvet-looking dress with white ribbons all over the front, and now Mami was braiding her hair and tucking little white plastic flowers into the crisscrosses.

—She looks like a present, like she got wrapped, I said to Mami.

Gisela stuck her tongue out at me, which was her latest brat thing to do that she thought would keep her cute. I gave her the finger and Mami yelled at us both to stop. Then Mami told me to change my clothes.

—You look like a gangster. Put on a nice shirt, she said.

—This *is* a nice shirt.

I had on my favorite threads: a Miami Hurricanes jersey, home colors, and my new size forty-two jeans, and I even had a belt on to keep them up.

—Pónte the shirt your abuela gave you for your birthday, the blue one with the long sleeves, and some decent pants. The black ones you use for church. Apúrate, que Papi's almost ready to go.

I changed without arguing, because we had this fight every year and every year I lost, even though wearing a long-sleeved shirt when it's eighty-five degrees outside on a Miami December night just to look nice for people I see two or three times a month anyways was crazy. Just when I had the last button done, Papi rushed by my room, keys in hand, ready to go. I could smell his Brut cologne coming and going. I threw on some Polo Sport, grabbed my Canes cap and the graduation pictures off my dresser, and followed him out to the truck.

He'd left the Tahoe right in front of the house. Papi climbed in first, careful not to touch anything but the handle to the door. He unlocked the rest of the doors from inside, and I got in and sat in my seat, behind his. My mom and Gisela came out of the house, and Mami, whose hands carried food, had Gisela digging in her purse to find the house keys.

I leaned forward, over my dad's right shoulder. His cologne was so much stronger than mine—his nose had to be burning from it.

—Hey, Papi, come on. Lemme take my car, I said.

—Manny, ya te lo dijo que we go *as a family*.

I sat back, crossed my arms, and slid down in the seat. My dad adjusted the mirrors even though no one had touched them. He looked in the rearview and ran both hands through his hair, then looked down at his fingernails. He looked at me in the reflection, but moved his eyes away quick when he noticed I'd caught him watching.

—Put on your seatbelt, he said.

Right then, I hated riding in the backseat more than anything. There was no room for my legs, even with the extra space Teresa not being there gave me. Back in the day, I got in trouble because Tere would tell my dad that my knees were touching hers, like I was doing it on purpose. I'd tell her, My legs are long, and she'd say, Well maybe you need to stop growing then. And Papi would yell, Stop fighting or I'll leave both of you out in the street to walk home.

I wanted him to turn on the radio so it could stop being all quiet. But I could hear Mami getting closer, whatever she was saying muffled by the closed car doors. She had a huge square aluminum dish full of congrí in her arms, and Gisela was carrying a big plate covered with foil in one of hers.

I finally said, But you let Teresa—

—Open the back for Mami, he said, not looking at me.

I opened my door and got out.

—Because your Tía Eva never gives these things back. Every year I ask her for them back and every year she forgets. Thank you, Papito, she said as I opened the back for her.

When I got back in the truck, my dad was looking for the Spanish radio station. I put on my seatbelt. My mom and sister climbed in.

—Don't touch the glass, he said to them.

Gisela held her hands out, fingers spread apart, then rested them on her lap. The locks slid shut.

—That food's not gonna spill back there, is it? Papi said.

—No, Manuel, vámonos, we're late already, Mami said. Her hair was smooth and down—she'd used the rollers after Tere took them out. She lowered the visor, looked in the little mirror, and started putting on her lipstick. When she was done, she stuck her whole finger in her mouth and pulled it out, and I had to look away out the window.

As we drove from our house, I saw my Integra parked under the aluminum roof, which is where Papi normally parked the truck. I'd left it parked on the other side of our fence, where I always leave it, but Papi had moved it without saying anything. Gisela tapped me on my hand, and when I looked at her, she stuck her tongue out at me. I turned back to the window and kept looking at the shade around my car until we turned off the block.

My dad started honking the horn as soon as we were in view of Tía Eva's house. By the time he parked, half the family was out there, looking at what was officially the first truck in the family. All the men smacked my dad on the back while my mom and my tías started hugging each other and saying how straight everyone's hair looked. I said wassup to my cousins, most of them standing outside over by the stereo, most of them my age more or less. My mom called me over to the porch and told me to say hello to everyone. She was so loca about it—pulling me away from my cousins by my shirt—I knew it was because she was nervous about Tere. I went around kissing everyone out there on the cheek. My mom had the graduation pictures in her hands. She passed them out, the older people getting the bigger copies. I said, Mom, wait til later, but she pinched me hard on the back of the arm, not wanting me to mess up her distraction.

—Ay, qué lindo! they all said when they got theirs.

—This is it, Manny, my Tía Yola said. She squeezed my shoulder with one hand and held the picture with the other. Her hair, still short and sprayed stiff, was bright yellow this year.

—Finally graduating, she said. You *know* we're all gonna be there.

—I know, Tía.

—With signs, Manny. *Big* signs. She winked.

—Can't wait, I said.

She snorted and pinched my ass.

—Look at this one, Mami said, showing my Tía Olivia a picture of me in a cap and gown with a stupid foam cutout saying 1997 in front of me. I'm holding onto the seven—so you can see my class ring—and I'm looking off into nothing.

Another Ay, qué lindo! I smiled at her to say thanks.

—Permiso, ladies, I said, escaping from the porch through the screen door. In the living room, right when you walked in, Tía Eva had the quinceañera pictures of all the tías in two rows on the wall, all of them with huge hair and crowns, the pictures yellower the older the tía was now. Under those, a new row of all the girl cousins at their fifteens, same crowns, same huge white dresses, Tere's picture the one starting off the row.

The guy cousins were separate—there weren't as many of us—wearing graduation stuff or suits, not even in the living room, but on the wall behind the dining room table. Tía would probably put the senior picture of me up next to my cousin Braulio, who graduated—barely—last year. In his, he's looking off at nothing, like in mine, and he's holding a fake rolled-up diploma in front of his chest like it means something. The graduation hat barely fits his big head even though his hair is mostly shaved in the picture. The background has these phony library books in it, stacks and stacks of them on shelves, which always makes me laugh because—even though he's my boy—Braulio is probably the stupidest of us cousins.

About two hundred pounds of food covered the tables in the dining room, and all of it drenched in mojito. It looked like a typical dinner at my house, but for about fifty people, and plus a lechón. There was yuca with onions, pollo asado—greasy and covered in garlic—fried plátanos, tostones looking like golden smashed flowers, about five dishes of congrí—my mom wasn't the only one who brought food even though Tía told them not to—my Tía Eva's famous frijoles, white rice, chicken salad with apples in it, chicken salad without apples in it, a plate full of cheese cubes, some pastelitos from La Habana Bakery, and at the end of one of the long tables, a cooler full of Cokes, Sprites, Heineken, and Michelob. I almost decided to forget the fork and just scoop rice up in my hands and shovel it in my mouth, but my Tía Yola came in looking for me.

—Oye Manny, she said, Y Teresa? Where is she?

—She's not here yet, I said without thinking. She's coming later though.

—She's coming with Ruben? Y tu papá let that happen? I gotta talk to your mother about this. And she ran back out to the porch.

The tías get pissed when they get left out of family gossip—even the kind that involves Papi and they know better than to ask—so though they knew that Ruben had asked my dad to marry Tere, and that my dad said it was okay as long as she finished her classes at MDCC first, they didn't know that Tere had been allowed to go to Ruben's house, which was a big deal to these old school Cubans for real. No one had ever escaped Noche Buena with my family. People came here—we'd cook a bigger pig, set another plate. I don't think we knew how to share family, even if it was just loaning them out until dinnertime.

—Y la niña? Tía Yola asked Mami as I came up behind them.

—Outside with the kids, she said, trying to play it off again.

—Not Gisela. La otra.

Mami stared at me, narrowing her eyes. The tías looked at me, then back at her.

—I guess Manny must have told you, Mami said.

—I didn't say—

—Teresa is at Ruben's house, she said. With his family until seven. Both of them will be here to have dinner with us.

She started shuffling the leftover pictures in her hands like that answer would be enough. I saw her fumble with them, almost drop them all, while the tías just looked at each other, their mouths open. Eva was the first to speak.

—He knows that once they get married, they have to come here, right?

My mom didn't say anything, just looked down at the pictures in her hand.

—Pero, Lourdes! How could you let her go to *his* Noche Buena, Eva said, more sad than angry. Then Yola started up with her crazy-ass religious stuff that everyone always nodded along with to her face but talked shit about when she'd leave a room.

—Even in the *Bible*, it says that a man will leave his family and join with the woman. *He* is supposed to come *here*. Not the other way around, she said.

—I know, but they are coming later, and I couldn't say no—his parents are so polite—and he's a very nice Cuban boy from a good family, Mami said.

—Then they should know better than to even ask! This from Eva.

—Raul stays here with Eva, Carlos comes here with Olivia, Manuel comes here with you, Eduardo used to come with me, Tía Yola said, counting off the couples on her fingers, even mentioning the ex-husband whose name we weren't supposed to say because our family didn't believe in divorce.

—Qué dijo Manuel about this? Tía Eva said.

Everyone looked out into the driveway at Papi, who was still out by the Tahoe, showing my Tío Raul how much space there was in the back when you lowered the seats. Papi was inside the truck on his knees, waving with both hands to get Tío Raul to crawl in next to him.

—She asked our permission, Mami said. She took big breaths through her nose, so big that I heard them.

—No lo puedo creer, Tía Yola said. I can't believe you let her go.

One of the abuelas sitting around the edge of the porch—old enough to sometimes be quiet—said in Spanish, It starts it off wrong. It starts it off all wrong.

My mom looked out at the driveway. Papi and Raul had shut the back doors and were inside the truck, crawling over the front seats to get out through the front doors.

—Discuss it with Teresa when she gets here, Mami said, holding the pictures up to her chest and pushing past me to get into the house. I followed her inside.

—I didn't mean to say anything, I said. She put down the pictures and picked up a plastic fork off the table, then she started mixing up a bowl of rice for no reason.

—But, I mean, they woulda noticed she wasn't here *eventually*, I said.

Now the rice was flying out of the bowl.

—I just want everyone to be happy, she said, still flipping rice everywhere. I try to tell your father, we have to let go, Teresita is a woman, but he wants her here. *I* want her here, too, but I'm not allowed to be happy. I never left *my* parents for someone *else's* family.

I almost said, Yeah but *Dad* did, but instead, I told her, Mami, calm down—cálmate. But she just ran over whatever I'd said.

—So I want Teresita to be happy, so I tell your father, Let her go with Ruben. Then I get here and it starts all over again. I'm always the bad one.

The plastic fork broke in her hand. She brought it up to her face, and at first I thought she was laughing, but instead she started to cry. It wasn't a stupid uncontrolled thing, like Tere when she wanted the world to know how Papi had destroyed her life by giving her a curfew or something. It was a cry that rolled out of her, like it had been pushing its way out a long time. Mami let the piece of fork in her hand fall on the floor.

I held her head and pulled her to my shirt, hugging her, and said, Shh, ya, ya. Her head was under my chin, her face near my armpit. She breathed in once real deep and then straightened up quick, wiping the mascara smudges from under her eyes and making sure she hadn't left stains on my good shirt. She smoothed down my goatee with her whole hand.

—At least you won't leave me, Manny, she said.

She looked at me with these watery eyes that made me think she believed what she'd just said, and I pretended to clear my throat so I could look somewhere else for a second.

After sniffling and wiping her nose on her hand, she jammed her stiff but straight hair behind her ears, checked to see that she still had both earrings in. Then she walked right past the people on the porch—looking at the truck ahead of them instead—back out to my dad in the driveway, with the Tahoe and the tíos, and asked him if he wanted something to drink. I felt like I should follow Mami and go talk to the guys with my dad, but I couldn't. I don't know if Mami said that because I didn't have a girlfriend, or because, if I had one, she thought I'd make this imaginary girl come to our Noche Buena instead of me going to hers. I picked up the piece of fork from the floor and pressed the broken edge into my thumb until the plastic snapped again.

No one mentioned Teresa—at least not in front of me or my mom—until she called at exactly seven o'clock. Tere pulled this all the time; she had to be home at a certain time, but that would actually be the time she'd leave wherever she was. But she'd *call* at that time to say she was on her way. And it always worked—my parents even thought she was more responsible for doing it, but I knew she was just buying herself more time. I tried this Tere-move once with Papi and he was like, Don't you start this shit with me. If I say midnight, I better hear the door locking at 11:59.

My luck, I'm the one who got the phone to hear, I'm on my way, we're leaving his parents' house now.

—Shit, Tere, I said into the receiver, turning away from the dining room and trying to cover my mouth. What the fuck are you trying to prove?

I heard her sigh hard, like she was tired. She said, Just tell Mami I'm on my way.

If I could have been sure that no one would see me, I would have slammed the phone back in its holder on the wall over and over again, so that Tere would have for sure known that I'd hung up on her. But with a family as on top of you as ours is—when they're like the heat in a car you've left parked in the sun—I knew some tía, or worse, Mami, would have been asking what the carajo did I think I was doing trying to break the phone. So instead, I tried to say something. I said, Tere, please. It's the fucking twenty-fourth.

—I *know* what day it is, Manny.

And then *she* hung up on *me*.

Mami had told everyone Tere and Ruben were coming at seven, so most people were out in the driveway again, waiting to ambush the car. Even my cousins had left their spots by the stereo—they'd heard, probably from me at some point, that Ruben drove a new Mustang.

When I finally hung up my end of the line and walked outside, Mami was the only one left on the porch, standing on her toes, trying to look way down the long block for some sign of any car. Her arms were crossed and she scratched with her hand at something on the back of her arm. The piece of skin looked raw already, like she'd been digging a hole there for hours. Papi was with the others in the driveway, leaning against the Tahoe, his back to the street.

Mami smiled at me and said, Was that the phone?

I let the screen door slam behind me and walked out to where Papi was at. I didn't wait until Tío Raul finished whatever it was he was saying. I put my hand on Papi's shoulder and leaned in. His cologne still hung around him, even with all the sweating he'd been doing showing off the truck. I told him, all quiet, about Tere's call.

Papi didn't even turn to face me after I'd told him. Instead, he stared straight ahead, at Mami alone on the porch. She still had her arms crossed, hugging herself. Papi swallowed hard—I saw his throat move—but other than that, it was like he'd been frozen in place. Tío Raul even waved his hands in front of Papi's eyes and said, Qué te pasa, Manuel?

Papi blinked, then came back to us and said to Tío Raul, Hermano, you look hungry. He walked up to the porch and turned around on the clay tile steps to face everyone. Mami stood a little further back, by the door, almost next to him.

—Ya, he said. I don't think we should wait. I'm hungry. ¡Vámonos, a comer!

He turned around and walked back into the house. I tried to glance at the road, but everyone started coming on to the porch and it blocked my view. I decided to be hungry, too, so I followed Papi in, opening the screen door again to let Mami in before me.

There was a lot of *What about Tere* as we sat around the two long tables. As I walked to the end where us guys always sat, I heard Tía Eva say we should wait longer, but Tía Yola said back, If Tere's own father doesn't want to wait, then there's no reason to let food get cold.

Papi sat near the head of the table, near Tío Raul and Tía Eva, waiting for my mom to bring him a little bit of everything on a plate, and she did. Gisela sat with the little cousins at a table we could see but that was more officially in the living room than the dining room. The kids ate lechón ribs and the crackly skin that Tío Raul separated for them as soon as they pulled the pig out of the pit, so that they got the best parts. When you graduate to the adult table, you trade in the best meat and skin, but for your sacrifice, you're now allowed beer. I sat next to my cousin Braulio, who was telling us how crappy his job at UPS was, but that he made mad money and was about to buy a new Civic or an Accord depending on the down payment and whether he got it new or used.

—Bro, he said to me, High school is bullshit. I been at UPS since I graduated, and I ain't used a damn thing I learned there for shit at work.

His fingers shined from grease, and I could see the pork moving over his tongue when he talked. I put down my fork, grabbed a chunk of meat from the aluminum pan in front of us with my fingers, threw it in my mouth, and started talking.

—You don't gotta read at work? I laughed. Or add shit?

He cracked up, and so did my other cousins, all of our mouths open wide, food shown off like engines at an auto show. Then my cousin Ricky said, Braulio can't *read*, and we smacked the table, almost choking, it was so funny.

Braulio coughed a little and said, Yeah, but that shit I had down in elementary. I could've started at UPS when I was twelve.

I reached past Braulio to grab some plátanos. Papi sat at the other end of the table—not looking even close to full—with his arm around Mami. Her hands were moving around, helping her tell some story, and Papi seemed to nod along with whatever she was saying. Mami paused for a second in the telling and Tía Yola busted out laughing. A piece of rice flew out of her mouth and onto the table right in front of Papi, and he sat up so quick to get away from it that he almost fell out of his chair. Mami lost it then, throwing her head back to laugh, her teeth in two wide rows, perfect except for all the fillings, her neck smooth and almost shining. By the time Papi straightened himself out, even he was smiling.

Braulio elbowed me and said, What you staring at?

I threw one of the oilier plátanos on his plate. It sat there in front of a slimy skid mark, looking like some delicious dead slug. I said, I'm staring at those ugly-ass old people down there.

We winked at each other and went back to our food. He knocked his shoulder into mine and said, Speaking of ugly-ass, where's this car you're supposed to have, bro?

I had wanted to say something about it all night, but at first I'd gotten stuck in the Teresa talk, and plus I knew it wasn't right to brag, especially when Braulio had been working hard to save money. But since someone had finally asked about something I *wanted* to talk about, I couldn't keep from giving a big stupid grin.

—Braulio, bro, I said, leaning back in my chair. This car. You have to see it.

I didn't know where to start: the rims, the sound system—how the speaker tube in the back was so big I barely had any trunk left—how a guy I met through the Auto Parts hooked me up with someone who cut the springs to drop the car for cheap, how Tere had wanted me to drive her to her night class with the windows down and the speakers rattling the whole frame.

But I didn't get a chance to tell Braulio anything, because someone started honking out in the driveway. Papi heard it too, and he looked my way. He pointed his fork at me, the end of it loaded with meat, then he pushed the food in his mouth. He kept on chewing like no one was leaning on a horn at the other side of the house. Mami kept talking, but Tía Eva looked past her toward the front door. People held on to the plates they'd been passing around.

Braulio said, mouth still full, I think your sister's here.

Tía Yola put her hands on the edge of the table and slid her chair back. It made a rough noise on the tile floor, and everyone—even the old abuelas hardly able to hear—watched her start to stand.

—I don't recognize that horn, Papi said to her. And if it's them, they can come in when they're ready. Sit down, sit, he said, waving her back into the table. Tell me you made flan for dessert.

She stood for a second, her hands still on the table, then smiled and said, Do I look like your mother?

Everyone started laughing again; Tía Yola always makes three different kinds of flan, more than we can ever eat in one night. But even with the loud voices, and even though people smacked the table and hit their plates with their forks, through all their noise I could still hear Ruben's horn.

His Mustang had a horn that matched the deep rumble of that monster engine—tough, and almost loud enough to throw off everything in the house. After a minute, the short nervous beeps became long steady presses. I looked at Papi, who was looking at his food.

Braulio licked his fork and said, That's Tere now for sure.

When the beep got so long that we could hardly ignore it—a full seven seconds of noise—I knew Braulio was right: that was Tere slamming on the horn. Ruben was new to this, and wouldn't want to do it, but Tere wouldn't be able to resist now that she was up in a front seat—not like when we were kids and someone brought a new car to Noche Buena. Those days, she always got trapped in the back. I remember she would even cry some years and promise not to pound on the steering wheel, but every time someone gave in, she'd prove them right, leaning on the horn with such force that it took two grownups to pry her off. She'd scream through the whole thing, but with a smile on the entire time. It was like she wanted people to see her and think, *Look at that little girl drive.* I looked down at my lap, at my crumpled napkin, greasy spots all over it like oil on a driveway.

Tía Yola finally leaned forward, her head low and her chest pressing on the table, almost spilling onto her plate, and said to Papi, Manuel, please.

He went for his water glass, avoiding Mami's stare.

Before Papi could say anything, I leaned over to Braulio and said, Watch my plate. I dropped my napkin on the table and pushed my chair out with the back of my legs. I thought it might tip over behind me, but I just kept walking away from the table, toward the front door. Papi said, Manny, wait, but I was already at the door, ready to open it, to jog out to Ruben and Teresa to tell them that their ride was pretty sweet.

Low Tide

They put their towels on the sand, which felt hard-packed beneath them. This part of Miami Beach was old, but like so much of Dade County, it still clung to the idea of glamour, choosing to ignore the years when police cars cruised right on the sand, pounding the shore worse than any natural wave. This half-dead beach is where Hector dropped their things. Yamila was surprised to see so many people there on a Wednesday, though she knew a weekend day would be much worse. The condition of coming on a weekday had made Hector finally agree to come to the beach at all; that, and her promise to show him that at thirty-nine, she could still pull off wearing a bikini. They found a spot not too close to any of the groups of teenagers, whose towels and boom boxes and shining bodies dotted the sand.

Hector's towel snapped in the wind as he put it down, and he walked around all four sides of it, pressing down on each corner with the toe from his bad leg, balancing his weight on the good one. Yamila used several of his mother's Tupperware—still full of food—to anchor the edges. Rap music competed with reggaetón and salsa, but from where they sat, they couldn't tell the music apart from the teenage voices yelling around them. Hector lowered himself to the ground, his track pants making plasticky noises as his legs fumbled against each other, until he was finally down with his legs stretched out in front of him. Yamila stared at his feet, at the yellowed toenails; she could see clearly the three-inch difference in leg length. He flexed the foot of the bad leg, so that the lengths evened out.

Yamila had wanted to ignore his limp when they'd first met almost a month before. She worked as a bank teller, and he'd come in to cash a check. She'd first thought, as he approached her counter, that he was limping on purpose, trying to walk with some style to make himself seem younger, but instead crossing over into parody. As he walked away from her, she'd changed her mind; maybe it was a blister. The next day, he came back with no checks to cash, but approached her window anyway to ask her out. And because she'd thought that maybe someone a decade older than her would have more money and be less likely to cheat on her, she said yes.

He'd told her about the polio, about his mother's refusal to have him vaccinated when it became available in Cuba, over their third margarita. She'd been too buzzed to keep quiet about her disgust with his mother for this, saying, *How could she—not my baby, if I had one.* He didn't recoil when she said this—in fact, he leaned in closer—and he told her more about his mother: how he still lived with her and how they fought like brother and sister, how she still made him lunch for work, that he could always hear where she was in the house because she never lifted her sandaled feet from the floor when she walked. Hector told Yamila that his mother's sheets were a bizarre neon pink, and her king-sized bed very high, and he wondered how she still managed to get into it without his help. *She doesn't know who's taking care of who,* he'd said. Yamila had let her hand smooth down the hair on his arm while he talked. She liked the idea that people watching them saw a *couple,* that when he joked with their waitress or handed the busboy a glass to save him the hassle of leaning across a table, they couldn't see his leg underneath; all they'd notice was this barely middle-aged woman with an older, maybe even charming man. She swore his eyes watered when he said, *I love my mother very much.* Close to drunk, she mentally undressed him until she got down to his legs, where she playfully pulled away the muscles of the shorter one like string cheese, until there was nothing but an old, knotted tree branch. She decided from then on that his walk was cute.

—Let's see that bikini you promised, Hector said. He must have smiled at her—the sun was behind him and Yamila could only make out his teeth.

—I don't know if you're ready, Yamila said. It is *scandalous.*

She gripped the bottom of her shirt as they both laughed. The cotton tank top was so tight on her that her breasts fumbled out from it. Her chest was a blur of freckles and age spots she played off as freckles. She had a tattoo of a tiger on the top of her left breast, but the tiger sagged with age, so that now its head looked too long for its body, its tail too short. She had gotten the tattoo on her twenty-eighth birthday, at the same time that she'd had the tattoo on her lower back, which had read *Felipe,* covered with a large, snarling panther. The most recent tattoos were on her right shoulder—two Chinese characters that she'd been told meant Beauty and Youth. The bikini was neon green, and it hung off Yamila from two knots—one behind her neck, where it tangled itself in the dark brown roots of her blond hair, and the other behind her back. She shook her hair loose from the tank top and readjusted her breasts in the triangles of material that covered them, trying to make them look firm.

—Holy wow, Hector said, but he had only looked at her for a second. All for me?

She leaned forward so that her breasts hung in the air in front of him as she wiggled out of her jeans. Her thin gold necklaces tangled together even more. One of these had a nameplate on it that she hadn't taken off since she was fifteen. All of her chains, she'd told Hector and many other people, were real gold.

—Maybe, she said.

After their second date, while sitting on her living room couch, she'd told him over a glass of rum how much she liked dancing. She was trying to convince him to take her to a club the next Saturday, and that's when he told her about the old house parties.

—My cousins would drag me to these things, he said. We weren't even fourteen. Of course there was dancing, and of course, *I* didn't ask girls to dance, but my cousins, they'd find the prettiest girl there and tell her to go ask *me,* that even though I was busy holding up the wall, I was actually the best dancer there.

Yamila had said, *Oh,* very softly and put her hand on his thigh, but Hector acted out the story with his arms like it was a favorite joke.

—Of course I say yes to her. I was in junior high, and we're talking older girls, high school girls.

He held his hands out in front of his chest to indicate breasts, and Yamila giggled and rested her glass on the coffee table.

—And it didn't matter what music they played—salsa, merengue, disco—I couldn't move the leg fast enough. So I'd step *all over* her feet. The girl would turn super red and limp away after one song. My cousins would laugh and laugh, but I was laughing harder. Because who had just danced with the prettiest girl there?

He leaned back and smirked as he shrugged his shoulders.

—My poor mother, he laughed, Always volunteering to chaperone. She called my cousins traitors. *Traitors*! She never figured it out—that I fell for it on purpose.

While he'd smiled to himself, Yamila had bent forward to shove her tongue in his mouth before he could say anything else.

Now at the beach, she balled up her jeans and threw them at his hairy stomach. Two more knots—one on each of her hips—secured the bottom of the bathing suit to her body. She sucked in her stomach and turned to her side, standing up on her toes. She lifted her arms and pulled her hair away from her face.

—Well? she said. Are you coming?

Hector sat up on his elbows. He looked out toward the ocean, his hair flapping.

—Me? No. No, I—I want to watch you in the water.

She cocked her head at him, about to pout. But a lyric blared from a boom box—a new song starting—and Yamila looked up because she could not make out what the rapper was saying. She glanced over to the closest group of people. Two teenage boys were picking up a girl by her ankles and shoulders, dragging her to the water, all of them laughing and screaming, the girl yelling, Rudy *stop* it! Another girl, left behind on the towel, yelled, *Puta bitches*! while smacking sand off of her legs. She spit three times before stretching back out.

Hector was still looking at the ocean. He said, Let me watch you walk. Go on.

She tiptoed over the Tupperware—getting a little sand on Hector's towel—bent down, and kissed him. She tasted Listerine, but the sun warmed her shoulders, so she put her hand on his back and pulled up, peeling his shirt from his sweaty skin. He raised his arms and she tugged it off him. He leaned back on his elbows again, his nipples spreading away from each other, melting across his chest toward the pockets of his armpits. She smiled at his expansive chest hair, at the hope she saw for the hair on his head in his bushy sideburns. She put the shirt to her nose, smelled the sea air mixed with his sweat and his musky cologne, and dropped the shirt on her towel.

She did not turn back to look at him as she went to the water. Two seagulls ran from a wave, barely leaving footprints for it to wash away. She watched them as she swayed her hips and willed her steps to float across the caked sand so that her butt would not jiggle.

The water glittered far out ahead of her. Two massive barges broke the horizon line, and a white cruise ship, only a faraway dot, floated away from shore. The foam of the water crowded around her ankles as her toes sank into softer sand. Her father had always said that going to Miami Beach in the summer was like going for a swim in piss, because the water was almost as hot as the air above it, but Yamila liked slipping into the warmth. So what if the ocean was a toilet? Hadn't they closed it down enough times because of sewage leaks, only to reopen it in time for the weekend, reporting that their tests had been wrong, that everything was fine? She walked further into the water, and when she was deep enough that it covered her waist, she turned around and waved to Hector while she squatted and peed. Hector waved back, and she snickered at her secret, feeling the water get even warmer around her. She dug a foot into the underwater mud, then pushed off of it as hard as she could to move to a fresh spot.

Wandering out further, where the water reached just below her chest, she dunked her whole head to wet her hair. When she was little, she used to hold her breath as long as she could and then suddenly explode out of the water, whipping her hair over her head in an arc like a sprinkler, so that when it landed, smacking her shoulders, it looked slick, molding itself into one long seaweed curl dripping down her back. She would do this over and over again with her younger sister, Yelisa, competing to see who was *la más sexy*—the standard being which of them, each turn, had flung her hair most like the model in the Presidente beer commercial. The winner got to sing the Presidente jingle in Spanish while pretending to seduce a bottle of beer. They called this game *Mermaids.* Yelisa would have her second baby—a boy, as far as doctors could tell—in three months.

When Yamila couldn't hold it any longer and finally charged up from under, her face rushing past bubbles of her own air, she half expected to see Yelisa there—bloated, floating better than ever, her hair sopping and already flung back—clearly the winner.

She lost track of Hector while feeling around on the ocean floor for seashells. She had her back to the shore, her chin up toward the sun to prevent a bad neck tan. She shut her eyes and held her arms straight out at her sides—as if she didn't want them to be wet anymore—dangling her already-wrinkled fingertips so that the pads of them just skimmed the water. Waves hardly lapped at her shoulders; aside from four teenagers a few yards away, splashing like animals, the water was tranquil. Her big toe hit a sharp rock—a broken piece of coral, she saw, once she grabbed it with her foot and brought it up—just barely buried in the silt. She heaved it away from her, in the direction of the teen couples, and it sank with a sound like a hard swallow.

She followed it down. Underwater, she could see only their legs, perfect and brown, kicking each other and hopping, treading even though the shallow depth didn't require it. One of the girls had toenails so red that Yamila could make each of them out even through all the silt kicked up.

Suddenly, she saw two sets of legs—the skinnier ones, both

of the girls—fly out of the water, as if scooped up by a colossal pelican. She thought, *Where is Hector*? Yamila flailed her arms, turning back around underwater, and came up for air.

It took her several seconds to find Hector, who was still staring out at the water from his towel, apparently in her direction. Her eyes stung from having them open underwater, and they teared to fix themselves, to cool off, but this only made the pain worse. She coughed a little, swallowing saltwater thick with spit, then waved at him with both arms. When he kept staring but did not wave back, she put her arms down and let her hands claw at her eyes. Behind her she heard the splash of flailing body parts. The burning eased, and she put her hand over her eyes to block out the sun. But Hector had moved away from their towels, a few yards over, standing near the girl the group of kids had left behind. He hovered over her, his weight clearly on his good leg. They seemed to be talking, or maybe he was flirting. Then Yamila snorted at herself for forgetting how this girl must see him—as someone's helpless dad, a lightly deformed old man wearing track pants on the beach. *My helpless old-man-dad*, Yamila thought, *Mine*. Her eyes hardly burned anymore. The girl sat up on her elbows and laughed at something Hector said, her chest bouncing. He squatted down next to her, his crippled leg unbending, pointing out toward the ocean.

From the water behind her came screaming. She turned and saw the two girls sitting on the shoulders of the boys, chicken fighting. The girls tucked their feet into their boyfriends' armpits, and their boyfriends grabbed their knees to stabilize them while the two girls shoved each other. Yamila had no idea who was winning. One of the girls slipped off her boy's shoulders a little and grabbed his whole head in her arms, like she would rip it off, until he backed far enough away from the other human pillar that she could readjust herself. Safe from the other team's threat, he let go of one of her knees to push up her butt, tucking her crotch into his neck.

The other boy said, Let's go already!

His hands pushed hills of water at them. His girl wobbled when he let her go to do this, but she kept herself from falling by holding out her arms.

The newly reassembled couple charged toward the other set

when they weren't expecting it. The boy on the bottom yelled, Nati, pay attention! as the team hurled into them. Nati, sent backwards by a slam to the shoulders, gave up any chance of staying up, using her hands instead to hold on to her bikini top straps. The other girl screamed at such a high pitch as she pushed that it rattled in her throat like a whistle. Her under-boy laughed, the whole time walking the girl forward, unrelenting in their attack.

Nati, as she was falling over, yelled, *Rudy-Rudy-Rudy*! until her voice crashed into the water. As she slipped off his shoulders, Nati kicked Rudy in the head with her heel. Her other foot caught him under his chin, kicking his head up while lodging in his neck. Rudy's legs rose out of the water, the rest of him dragged under with Nati. The winning team—the girl still perched on her boy—said together, Oh shit. Yamila looked back and saw that Hector had been following the whole thing.

When Rudy came back up he had his fingers in his mouth, feeling for his tongue. His other hand was rubbing the back of his head as if trying to make it shine. He removed his hand and spit in it, and Yamila saw, along with all his friends, a dark pink arc spew from his lips.

—Fucking shit, Nati, he said.

Nati surfaced, but at first couldn't do anything but cough. Between breaths she said, *Baby*? She put her arms up to hug him from behind, but he splashed and turned around, pushing her away. Again she said, laughing a little, Baby. Then she said, I'm sorry, you okay?

—I'm bleeding, he yelled, You kicked me!

The other girl slid down from her boyfriend's shoulders, bobbing in the water behind him. Yamila thought the band of them looked so fresh, so bronze, that she wished a wave would crash over them, that the ocean would somehow split them all apart.

—Calm down, the girl said, gliding toward Nati.

—I'm fucking *bleeding*, he said, pointing both hands toward his mouth.

Nati said, It was an accident, baby, please. She tried to hug his arm, but as soon as she touched the top muscles, the arm sprung away from her and smacked the water. Rudy faced shore and dove back underwater while the others rubbed salt from their eyes.

Yamila saw his body approaching, a long shadow in front of her.

He was not so deep that she couldn't make out each of his limbs, all of them tanned and hairless. His legs kicked behind him, spilling out of his crimson swimming trunks, which hung down to his knees. The current tugged them down as his wide strokes pulled him through the water, revealing a line of peach below the waistband—the beginning of his real color. As he swam by, still in his dive away from his friends, Yamila saw his calves, each like a square-cut jewel, working to move him. She thought his legs were twice the thickness of her own, that he must work out, how easy it must be for him to move fast through the water—with legs like those, he could swim anywhere in no time. As he passed her, his feet only inches away—she could even make out yellow calluses on his heels—she thought, without looking up from the boy, maybe that's why Hector wouldn't join her in the water. Maybe Hector, with his withered baby-leg, could not swim.

Rudy's feet finally broke the surface as he kicked, sending blades of water at Yamila. She had been looking down right at him with her mouth open, and the water stung as it flooded her nose and throat. Rudy stopped and stood up in the water, small trickles falling down his chest like dozens of tiny rivers suddenly drying out. She thought maybe he played football for his high school team. He looked down at himself when he saw Yamila staring at his nipples.

—Sorry, lady, he said.

Yamila half-smiled and smoothed back the wet chunks of hair dangling around her face. Rudy spit into his hand and inspected the red puddle. He dunked his hand underwater to rinse it, looking at the gold chains around Yamila's neck, then scowled at the group before licking his lips. Yamila cleared her throat and joked, Lady? Who, me? but he plunged back below the surface and headed for land.

The other girl said, Forget it, Nati, he's just being pissy.

Yamila watched Rudy swim away, and when she finally looked past him, at the shore, she saw Hector, his body and leg inches from the group's blanket. Yamila dove underwater, pushing herself toward the beach.

Rudy had already planted himself on his towel by the time Yamila reached the shore. He stretched out just a few feet from Hector and the girl, sitting up and spitting in the sand every few seconds. Rudy's towel was near a blue cooler that Yamila could see, as she came closer, had beer bottles in it, even though they were not allowed on the beach. The girl laughed at something else and Yamila sucked in her stomach, but Hector was still bent over the girl and did not see her coming.

—No no, the girl said to Hector, It's Senior *Skip* Day. Class of '97, 97 days til graduation, so you skip that day. It's Hialeah Lakes High tradition.

Before Hector could say anything, Yamila said, Hello? like she was answering a phone.

—Oh hey! the girl said. She smiled at Hector. Is this your wife?

Hector jammed his fingers into the sand and didn't answer.

—I'm his girlfriend, Yamila said. She did not look back at Hector, but looked directly at the girl on the towel. Her body glistened, unconsciously posed. She had a bar through her belly button—a piercing Yamila had once considered. The girl squinted and smiled at Yamila so brightly that Yamila thought she might have to smack her.

—Girlfriend, huh? She cocked her head. Weird, she said.

—Why is that weird? Yamila put her hands on her hips again. Her fingers twitched.

The girl shrugged her shoulders. I dunno, she said, I *guess* it's not.

Yamila could not tell if the girl was blushing, or if her cheeks had started to burn. The girl bit her lip, then gave Yamila a straight-on grin.

—*Girlfriend* is such a weird word anyways, the girl said. She looked away, the red deepening. She said, I mean, think about it, right?

Rudy growled to wrangle up more spit. When the clot joined its predecessors in the sand, he said, Ana, lemme get the suntan lotion.

She reached over to her bag and tossed him a brown tube. He caught it and squeezed out a handful of what could have been butter. He rubbed the cream on himself in wide circles, admiring his own chest. Between the spikes the water had combed into his close-shaven hair, Yamila could see his scalp. Still, she could not imagine a future where this gorgeous thing was bald. When he looked up from his torso inspection, he caught Yamila's stare. He tossed the tube toward Ana and turned to his side, grunting as he faced the sun, his back to them. She looked at Hector, who had also followed Rudy's moves, and took in the glint of his bald spot. She thought of knocking him over.

Hector cleared his throat again and tried to stand. He said, Well. We better—

Yamila heard his knee crack, a sound like rocks rubbing together. He fell forward a little and propped his body up with his elbows.

—Oh man, did your leg fall asleep? Ana said. I *hate* when that happens.

Yamila crossed her arms, waiting for Hector to answer. She returned Ana's stupid smile with one of her own, cocking her head so that the girl would feel comfortable enough to maybe ask some questions.

Hector said, Yeah, me too. It'll wake up in a second.

Yamila tightened her grip around herself, squeezing her own biceps. Hector was bent over, both hands in the sand, trying to right himself. He gnashed his teeth and was soaked with so much sweat it looked like he'd been swimming. As he struggled up, the legs of his track pants rubbed together and sounded like they were being shredded. He seemed stuck in a half-split. Yamila uncrossed her arms, rolled her eyes, and put out her hand.

—Here, she said.

Hector turned his face, his hair flopping forward over one eye. He gritted his teeth like he would bite off her fingers if she came closer.

—I'm fine, he said. Relax, huh?

He balanced himself with one hand so he could use his other to push hers away. It wasn't a hard push, but Yamila took a step back. Ana looked between them and pouted.

Hector finally stood up as straight as he could, slapping the sand away from his hands and pants. He patted his hair back in place. He looked down at Ana and smiled, but he did not smile at Yamila. He rested his hands on his lower back and stared past her, out toward the water. Ana shrugged.

Yamila heard Rudy spit again, this time over and over, like he had a hair on his tongue. Ana shifted on her towel, stretching out her legs and flexing her toes, making her stomach look even flatter, so Yamila sucked in her gut again. She tossed her wet hair, but there was hardly any breeze to make it look seductive. She knew it didn't matter what she looked like, because both Hector and Rudy still refused to face her, even as the sun glinted off her nameplate, her necklaces, even as her hair dripped and she sang the Presidente beer jingle all the way through in her head.

Yamila finally said to Hector, Why don't you take off those silly pants and come into the water? Why don't you come swim with me?

That got him to see her. He opened his eyes wide. The muscles in his jaw tightened, and he puffed out his chest. His hands dropped to his sides in a surrender, but Yamila kept going.

—Come on. And who wears track pants at the beach? Yamila smiled at Ana. Am I right?

—True. You'll get stuck with ugly white legs, Ana said.

Rudy laughed at something down the beach.

Yamila said, Let them get some sun.

Ana leaned forward and tugged on the ankle of his pants. Yamila had to hold herself back from stepping on the girl's hand, squashing it like a spider. Instead, she said, Yeah, go swim.

Hector coughed a little into his hand. He said he hated the ocean.

—Nobody *hates* the ocean, Ana said.

Hector said he did.

Rudy finally looked back at them. He said, Bro, only losers hate the ocean.

It was the smartest thing Yamila had ever heard a boy like Rudy say. He leaned back on his towel, spit once more, and, seeing that the liquid was finally clear, nodded his head once.

—You hear that, Hector? Yamila said. She stuck her finger in the waistband of his track pants, pulled the waistband out, then let it smack back on him. He jumped at the sting. He ran his palm over his hair, both slick with sweat, and she almost started swaying to the Presidente jingle—she felt that close to winning.

—Yeah, bro, Rudy said. Go swim with your old lady.

Yamila sucked in air through her nose; he could not have meant her. She waited for him to wink at her—something to let her in on his joke—but he just bobbed his head in rhythm with a song she didn't recognize on a station she never listened to. Ana did not slug Rudy's arm, or say *She's not old,* or even suck her teeth at him. She defended no one. She only said, Yeah, just look at that water! while staring ahead of her at the ancient ocean.

The comeback couldn't form in her head; Hector's mouth twisted in a smile, a face as bright as if Ana had decided to go topless. Showing all his teeth, he watched Yamila as he undid the knot holding up his pants. He pushed them down from his waist and began to move side to side once he got them around his knees, dancing a fast merengue. Underneath the track pants, he wore only boxers, thin white ones with red pinstripes. Now she was sure that even though he'd agreed to go to the beach, he'd never planned to go near the water with her; he knew what he was falling for, so he'd left behind his trunks on purpose.

He kept up his sidestepping dance, looking almost graceful, until the pants were in a pile at his feet. Yamila looked at his bad leg, the knee clinging to the other bones like a wad of gum, but the curls of black hair made the leg look sturdy. He bent down and picked up the pants, shaking the sand from them.

Yamila heard Rudy say, And then, after she smacked the back of my head, she kicked me in the neck. Nati is fucking vicious.

Hector's legs did not match his sun-spotted chest and shoulders. He adjusted his boxers and stretched his arms over his head. She saw the toes on his good foot kneading the sand. Hector threw the pants at Yamila's stomach, breaking her stare. She barely caught them.

—You hold on to those, he said. My turn to swim.

Hector walked past Yamila to the water, his steps falling in with the beat of a far-off song, the boxers letting the world see the crooked dance. Yamila waited for the girl to say, *What's wrong with his leg*? but Ana wasn't even watching him anymore. She was sitting up, cross-legged, listening to Rudy as he reenacted the chicken fight with two beer bottles from the cooler.

But Rudy, Ana said, You can't be mad, she did it by accident. It's not the same as hurting you on purpose.

Yamila let Hector's pants spill out of her hands to the sand. The further away he walked, the more the jerks of his steps turned into a swagger. She saw in his stride the careful rhythm of his feet, a gait he'd choreographed over years, the bad leg dragging itself into place just in time to keep him going. Saltwater dripped from the ends of her hair, splattering her shoulders and chest. With her towel still stretched out on the sand, she had nothing to dry off with, and she shook from the cold, the sun doing little to keep her warm now. Her teeth chattered loudly in her head, drowning out Rudy's distorted account of the chicken fight. Shudders rocked her vision, shaking it so much she wasn't sure if the man she watched crash into the water was still Hector. She had nothing but a trembling picture of a man on his back, his arms wrenching his body away from her as he floated into an empty, ready ocean.

Men Who Punched Me in the Face

The other guys on the football team called him Vick the Dick, and he said it was because he had a huge one, but I wouldn't have known then since his was the first one I ever saw. Victor was half Cuban—half decent, my dad used to say—and half some sort of Venezuelan-Ecuadorian mix. My mother declared him The Best Looking Guy To Ever Talk To Me three minutes after meeting him. He had this hard-line chin and perfect eyebrows that looked like a professional Hialeah beautician had sculpted them. He never got carded when he ordered beer at El Rey Pizza. He could grow a beard in two hours. After a game, he smelled so much like man sweat and dirt that I worried just smelling him would make me pregnant. He was light brown but close enough to white that my abuela didn't hate him. He bit his nails down so much that skin grew over top of them, so he'd chew on that until he ripped off spit-able hunks. Sometimes I worried that he'd get germs in me because his hands were so raw from how he ate them, but that was the kind of thing I never said to him because I didn't want him to realize we didn't belong together.

A few hours before our first date, I couldn't stop noticing in the mirror that I was growing a mustache, or at least, the shadow of one. The dark hair on my arms had magically migrated to my face, and in the light of the bathroom, it seemed more pronounced than ever. And because I thought that maybe Victor might kiss me—I held unreasonably optimistic ideas about love before meeting him—I went through my mom's medicine drawer and found her Nair. After wiping the caked cream from the ridge of the bottle, I applied a thick, even layer over my entire face, covering everything except my forehead and nose just to make sure I didn't miss a hair. I was either too sensitive or no good at telling time; either way, the cream burned everything, red blotches blending in with the light purple scars of my old zits. Later I tried to hide what I'd done by dragging a sponge soaked with foundation across my stinging skin.

Victor did not say *What happened to your face*? until we left the movie, like that was the first time that night he actually saw me. I said, I must be allergic to something.

He said, I hope it's not me, and he finally kissed me, in front of everyone leaving the theater, messed up skin and everything. That moment, coming right at the beginning of Us, made me think for a long time he was sweeter than he really was.

To be honest, it was closer to a slap than a punch, and I only stayed with him afterward because that's what I kept telling myself: it was a slap, not a punch, and every time I pictured it, his fingers opened up more, my memory making it over into something I could allow. I told myself Victor was a very emotional kind of person—the rush that made him hit me was the same one that made him throw me over his shoulder in the school hallway and carry me to my next class. And he started off being okay with me not wanting to have sex until marriage. He took it upon himself to teach me how to give blowjobs. I was sixteen and way behind most of the girls in my grade at Hialeah Lakes High. Part of me was relieved to get it over with, and with a guy who other girls wanted and who didn't mind being my tutor. Victor was not smart or creative, but he lifted women off the ground when he hugged them and talked about how much he loved his mother in front of my mother. Mami liked him so much she'd lie to my dad about the level of parental supervision wherever we were going and let us go out without a chaperone, which excited and terrified me at the same time. Only a handful of us girls in the neighborhood still had these throwback parents—members of the Chaperone Guild that collapsed once we all turned twenty and moved out amidst threats we could never come back—and that meant guys rarely talked to us for very long. But for some reason, Mami covered for Victor—she *wanted* us to be alone together. By our five-month anniversary, I was making myself vomit before every date for fear of throwing up on him when he'd come, which is what happened the first time, in the backseat of his car, and what made him hit me. The second after he did it, he looked at his own hand, and his dark eyes got huge. He said, *Oh baby, I'm so sorry, I'm so fucking sorry,* and I thought he might cry. He pulled me to his chest, even kissed me on the mouth, with his tongue, and I could taste his musty spit through the vomit and semen. His sweat-slicked chest hair scratched my face as he breathed, and I started negotiating with myself: I'd never had a real boyfriend before him, at least not one my mom willingly lied to my dad about when it came to a chaperone. By then it was clear that my mom loved Victor, and at that age I still thought she knew better than me when it came to love.

After Victor dropped me off, I sat outside my house until the red welt melted so my mom wouldn't ask any questions.

The weekend after the slap, to prove that he loved me, Victor took me to meet his dad. He hadn't seen him in three years, not since his dad was moved from his old apartment on North Miami Beach to a hospital complex where he couldn't wander off and get put in jail for breaking into people's homes he mistook for his own.

The nurse showed us to Victor's dad's room. He sat by the window, watching the rain smear the glass. He was bald on top, which I wasn't expecting, and he was much darker than Victor. He wore a plaid shirt tucked into black pants held up by a brown leather belt. He turned around and stood by the window. He was bulky, but not fat, and one of his feet looked permanently bent outward, like it would go left with or without him. He was handsome, looking very much like Victor until he smiled, a movement that made the sagging skin beneath his eyes puff out like the red flash of a lizard's throat. One of his front teeth was black, and the lower ones crowded together in a stampede to escape his mouth.

The nurse said, in Spanish, Rolando, you have some visitors.

Once she explained who we were, Victor's dad seemed thrilled to have a son—a son with a girlfriend!—and he talked to me about being a boxer in Venezuela, which Victor later told me was true. Victor's dad didn't speak English anymore, so he spoke to us only in Spanish, which Victor, like a lot of people our age, never really learned. I did most of the talking between them. Victor's dad asked every few minutes about Luz, Victor's mom. Victor tried, in his broken Spanish, to talk instead about his older brothers, Rolando Junior and Paul, but his dad couldn't place the names and would always go back to asking us when Luz was coming. Victor said, I—I don't know.

Victor's dad looked at me, the scary smile creeping out, and said, *She very pretty*, the English words surprising all three of us.

Victor said, Who? Her? Or Mom? but Rolando just sat there, his gaze drifting down to my chest, his smile gone.

As I drove us back to our neighborhood, windshield wipers working frantically in a typical Miami afternoon thunderstorm, I looked at Victor at a red light, and even though he was hiding his face from me and saying, *Come on, don't look at me, huh*? I saw what Victor looked like when he *really* cried.

We stayed together almost six more months after he hit me. We broke up before he moved away for school. He ended up sort of going to college (never full time, never finished) and while he was there, he met this American girl who would have sex with him without being married, which, contrary to all Cuban logic, got him to eventually marry her once she graduated. He called me two weeks before the wedding to thank me, *thank* me, for teaching him so much, that he learned a lot from me about what makes a man, that he was sorry he was cruel about the blowjobs and the sex, that he'd been a dick. He said into my answering machine, *You know, Vick the Dick,* and laughed a little, like his name was an excuse. I stood over the machine as he left the message and deleted it the minute he was done.

One of the few people from Hialeah Lakes High who I still talk to went to the wedding. She told me, when I saw her at La Habana Bakery days later, that his *Americana* wife, Vicky (Victor and Vicky—it made me want to throw up all over again), looked like a tulle factory explosion walking down the aisle, that she had the balls to wear white when everyone there knew she didn't deserve it, and that she didn't eat any of the wedding cake because of her diabetes. Something about this last fact thrilled me, this knowledge that for the rest of his life Victor would be with a woman who couldn't eat whatever she wanted. I bought a whole box of señoritas, picking only the ones with piles of frosting and heavy cream and fruit fillings. I ate every single one of them that night in my apartment, gorging myself and licking powdered sugar from my fingers, laughing when cream filling shot out from the pastries onto my chin. I ate and ate until my stomach felt like it would burst.

Some random guy named—I think—Carl took a swing at me once in a club called Karma. But he mostly missed and instead splashed my sequined halter top—on which I had spent half my paycheck—with a drink called Liquid Cocaine that tasted like cinnamon and stained like blood. This was one of those low points, way after Victor, after other guys, after I'd moved out of my parents' house and gotten the secretary job at UPI construction, which let me make some non–high school friends who did more than sit around and smoke weed. One Liquid Cocaine cost twelve dollars, but it got you messed up fast enough to be worth the price, and getting messed up had become my new definition of *weekend.*

Carl was the only white guy on the dance floor that night. He had a shaved head and was so pale he looked almost see-through in the club's strobe lights. After downing my second Liquid Cocaine, Carl glided over, pulled me off my bar stool, and handed me his drink. An hour later, we were still locked together. My friend Manny, a nice guy from UPI who'd invited me to Karma in the first place, glared at us from the bar.

Carl's sweat soaked through his mesh shirt, making the net of fabric cling to his nipples, which were at eye level for me, even with my strappy heels. He slid two of his fingers between my skirt's waistband and my stomach, pulling it down a little. I closed my eyes and threw my head back and kept dancing. Someone seized my elbow from behind me. I turned and there was Manny, dragging me from the dance floor to the bathrooms.

In that too-bright hallway, he screamed over some raging techno song, What the fuck are you doing, Sandra?

I slurred, Shit, Manny. I can handle myself.

I leaned against the wall to keep Manny from swaying in front of me.

Carl busted out from the throng of people on the dance floor and stormed toward us, his mesh shirt climbing up his perfect abs like it was taking itself off. His belly button was a tight knot with a patch of curly blond hair dripping down from it, disappearing into his red pants. In the lights near the bathroom, I saw how much we were sweating; Manny's hair had wilted and was plastered to his forehead, my own hair clung to my neck and shoulders like I'd dunked my head in water, and pearls of sweat dressed Carl's upper lip, streams running from the top of his head down the sides of his face, down his neck, like he was melting. I shoved out my chest and smiled at both of them. Carl's head turned from me to Manny then back to me.

Carl said, Bro, why don't you get up off my woman?

I felt like I was about to puke up Liquid Cocaines, so I gulped hard and breathed through my nose, smelling the earthy stink of all three of us. Manny looked down at the ground, which was inexplicably muddy and dotted with multicolored strips of paper. He leaned against the wall. Flecks of light from the dance floor decorated his face like moving makeup. Little pimples had sprouted between his eyebrows, the milky tops of them glowing—ingrown hairs, I thought, from where he let me pluck the strays threatening to unite his brows. I'd done it at work the day before, pulling the tweezers from my purse as he squatted by my desk during his break. He'd rested his chin in my palm and said, Don't hurt me, okay?

Manny squeezed his eyes shut like he was trying to erase me from his night and I felt bad just then for not dancing with him—I felt bad for wanting to dance with this stranger Carl over Manny, who I knew liked me, who had tried to do things the right way by being my friend first. But that obvious courting—his practiced conversations about concerts he thought I might want to go to, the way he asked about my mom even when he hadn't met her yet—is what did him in, what made that version of me decide he was too nice, not aggressive *enough*, not my type.

I stepped toward him but tripped a little on the mud-soaked paper and started falling in Carl's direction. Both reached out to help me, but I grabbed onto Manny's arm with my free hand, stared up at his face, and said, Can you take me home?

Carl grabbed me by the shoulder, standing me up straight again, but then pulled his other arm far back and blasted his fist at me. I put my hand up in time to get him to knock the drink out of it on the way to my face. The plastic cup flew at me. Manny tried to bat it away but was a little slow, which made him hit the guy's hand instead, so that Carl's fist landed not in the middle of my face but at my jaw, his knuckles grazing my neck. Manny grabbed the top of my head and pushed it down, out of the way of the second swing, and then dragged my drunk ass down the hallway and back across the dance floor, my boobs coated in sticky reddish punch. When we got outside, the bouncer said, Is there a problem?

Manny, always good on his feet at work, said, No, no, she just needed some air.

He put his arm around me and made me walk fast, away from the club's long-lined entrance, my ankles trying to escape my shoes and bending like chewed-on straws. I turned to look at the bouncer, and he was shaking his head no and laughing, mumbling something into the face-hugging microphone that seemed to grow out of his ear. He held the end of a velvet rope in his hand and clicked it to the post behind him, sealing all the beautiful people inside as we ran from Carl, or from security, neither of which had bothered to follow us.

After that night, Manny's attempts to get with me trailed off.

He stopped dropping by my desk during his breaks, stopped asking me what I planned to get into over the weekend. A few weeks later, he quit working at UPI to go back to school, didn't even tell me about it until the day before he left for good. I asked him out then, told him we had to celebrate him getting out of that shitty office, but he said no thanks, told me he was tired of the same scene. Wasn't I, he asked, getting tired of drinking my brains out? We stopped talking after that.

I blamed myself for his quitting, but was secretly impressed with myself for having such an effect on a guy—I had the capacity to ruin someone. But then I learned he'd met a girl at some new church he got into and married her four months later. From God, his mom told my mom. This new girl was sent to him from God. My mom suggested we go to this church and find someone for me. I stopped talking to her for a while, too.

Rudy Torrez. He didn't always hit *me*—it started with the walls, when we moved in together, his fist making circles in the plaster of our apartment like he'd gone crazy trying to hang a frame. But what hurt more than any punch was his lying, which he did all the time and about everything. He lied about when his parents came from Cuba because he didn't want me to know it was on the Mariel boatlift. He lied that his mom was a nurse at Baptist Hospital when I told him I was thinking of going to nursing school, and weeks later he told me she owned a bakery in Hialeah when I said I had a weakness for guava pastelitos. Of course I called him out on this, and he said she did both, but then changed his mind and said I must have misremembered what he said. Even though we were together for three years, I never really knew where he worked, though he always had money. When we talked about our future, he would say he wanted to go to fireman training, or police training, or another time he said he was looking into being a veterinary assistant. For three months, he worked "in computers" and managed to bring home pieces of plastic he could never get to work together. He made a lot of his money through insurance scamming, pretending to steal cars or boats from people who needed the cash for something else. But he always thought of

these as his side jobs, and these side jobs are what finally let him save up enough to buy me a ring.

Rudy hit me the most, probably because we were together a year and a half before it even started. I was twenty-eight by then and I couldn't throw that time away, especially with a ring on my finger and a mom asking about weddings and grandbabies. Once me and Rudy celebrated our year anniversary, my mom wouldn't stop saying how she had two kids by the time she was my age, how every cousin was married but me.

One night, to shut my mom up about how lucky I was to have Rudy, I took her with me to follow him when he left after one of our fights. Usually when I followed him, he'd go to his mother's house to change clothes, and then hit the grimier South Beach bars to buy drinks with names like *Slutty Chicken* and *Raging Orgasm* for younger versions of me. This night started out the same as usual. I turned off my car lights and parked down the street from Rudy's mother's house, only a few blocks from where my own parents lived.

Mami said, What is he doing here? I said, Watch.

Rudy came out not even ten minutes later, wearing black pants with silver lines running down them, and a silk silver button-down shirt that I knew he would sweat through in five minutes or less. His hair was gelled back and he'd switched out the standard hoops he wore in his ears for over-sized diamond studs. The car's lights blinked when he unlocked its doors.

Mami said, What is *this*?

I handed her a baseball cap and a pair of sunglasses, even though it was dark out, and once I'd tucked all my hair beneath a bandana and hung an American flag and a pair of blue baby shoes from the rearview mirror to disguise my car, we pulled out after him.

Rudy led us to a neighborhood off the expressway, four exits north of where we lived, where brand new palm trees propped up by giant toothpicks lined every street. None of the windows had bars on them, and all the houses were painted different shades of peach; each of them had the same exact lawn in front of it, matching squares of green felt. The neighborhood's roads had all these useless turns in them to make it seem bigger and better than it was—not like our blocks in Hialeah, which were on a clean grid promising to prove you stupid if you got lost.

I turned off the headlights and nudged the car just past one of the useless turns, just enough to see where he'd parked. I rubbed the steering wheel, making little black rolls of sweaty skin peel from my palms. I wiped them off on my jeans. Rudy flipped down the visor and checked his hair and eyebrows one last time, then sprung out of the car, slamming its door and strutting up the driveway. He brushed off his shoulders before pressing the doorbell with his whole fist.

Mami said, This isn't happening, it can't be happening. I shushed her.

A woman came out wearing a blue nightgown, and behind her stood another woman, younger and dressed in a short cream skirt with a slit up one side. Her blouse was in the shape of a huge butterfly, the glittered wings reaching high enough to cover the front and some of the side of her breasts. The butterfly fastened itself to her torso with only three silky cords, which crisscrossed each other like the wrapping on a butcher-bought ham. Rudy kissed the older woman's cheek first, then took the hand of the younger one, pulled her from the front step, and kissed her cheek, too. The older woman said something. Rudy nodded and said something back, and all three of them laughed. I pushed the button to unlock the car doors, my finger shaking on its grooved surface, and when I turned to Mami, she was facing me, hat off, breathing hard through her nose, hand already on the door latch.

Mami was the first to say anything. She screamed toward the house as we ran, our feet sinking into the mud of the little lawns.

—You son of a bitch, you puta bitch comemierda maricón!

She flailed her arms as she ran, and I grabbed them and pinned them behind her as we got to the front step. The girl clutched Rudy's hand and said, *Rudy*? But the woman in the nightgown pulled her by the arm, tugging her closer to the front door, leaving Rudy on the step by himself.

—I can't *believe* this, I yelled. I can't—

But Mami took over, escaping from me and shoving her long crooked fingers right in the middle of Rudy's chest.

—You say you're going to get diapers and *this* is where you really go? Mami said.

The butterfly shirt girl read my mind and said, Diapers? *What*?

Rudy and I both stared at my mom like she was crazy. She kept yelling, but not at Rudy—at the girl and her mom.

—Leaving my poor daughter alone with Little Rudy on a Friday night to go out when you can't even afford your car payments, when she has to pawn her wedding diamond so that you can get gas!

I turned my engagement ring with my thumb and hugged the little stone in my palm. I crossed my arms to look mad and bit my lip. I said, *Poor Little Rudy,* and held my head in my unringed hand.

Rudy's head ping-ponged between the two mother-daughter sets so fast it looked like he was trying to shake his jaw loose from the rest of his face.

—They're lying, he said. Nuria, he said to the girl, they're lying!

—Nuria! Mami yelled, Ay Dios mío in heaven and earth.

Mami turned around to face me and said again, Nuria! Her eyes widened and she tilted her head so slightly that only I knew what it meant. I started to cry.

—Rudy, you maricón, you go and find *another* girl named Nuria to cheat on *your wife* Nuria with?

Mami sounded so genuinely shocked I was almost convinced I had a new name.

—Her name is Sandra! he yelled, pointing at me. Sandra Ortiz! She's not my wife and I don't got any kids—with her or no one!

The other women gasped, and my mom's mouth hung open. The girl pulled at her finger, her dyed blond hair shaking with her jerky movements. Her mother held onto each of her shoulders.

Mami whispered, How dare you.

I pushed her out of the way and rushed Rudy. I smacked him on the side of his head, hopping a little to reach it. He put his hands up to protect himself and said, *Sandra, relax, please.* But I kept smacking him on his arms and shoulders as fast and hard as I could. A car passed by and honked once but kept going. My hands became fists, the slaps turning into punches. I said, *Puta, how do you like it* through my teeth, thinking no one heard it but me and Rudy. My hair flew in my mouth and made me cough. I let the spit drip from my chin and fly all over his clean shirt; the threads landed on the silver silk, leaving dark slashes. I kept hitting him until he crouched down on the wet lawn. The front door of Nuria's house slammed shut, and after that, through my smacks and sobs, I heard half a dozen locks slide and click into place. When I stepped back, he had red marks all over his arms, which he kept up, ready for more. I knew it couldn't have really hurt—I'm not very strong—and they were the kind of blows that punished kids, the kind felt way more by my imaginary Little Rudy, but my hands burned, and they shook. The stone from my ring had left scratches on Rudy's arms.

A small gold ring with a water-colored stone rested on the doormat where the real Nuria had left it before shutting all of us out.

I heard the smack of flip-flops on feet and turned around. Mami sprinted toward my car, yelling, *Dios mío* the whole way there. I waited for Rudy to say, *Sandra,* and put his arm out for me to help him up, to come back to me the way I had to him, but he just sat there like a boy thrown off a swing set, legs splayed out under him. I looked at the houses surrounding us. Neighbors had not turned on their lights. No one stood in doorways with phones in hand. The people living in that neighborhood north of us did not want our drama, did not see it as going along with the territory. They were smarter than me—smart enough to stay away. They knew that was the only move that guaranteed this never happened again. Nuria's street was nothing like where I lived. But at least now I was ready to stay away, too.

I left Rudy there and ran after Mami, who was trying to start the car from the passenger seat. I slid behind the wheel, taking the keys from her. Puddles of mascara lapped beneath her eyes, and her nose and mouth looked bloated from crying.

As I drove away—making a U-turn in the middle of the street to avoid passing Rudy—Mom blubbered through sob-swelled lips, I had to lie like that, I *had* to exaggerate the story, because him cheating is not enough to impress anybody.

I wiped underneath my eyes with the side of my hand. I shushed her. She looked at her empty hands in her lap. She said, Just cheating doesn't explain throwing it all away.

—It wasn't just fucking cheating, Mami! I screamed.

I cried harder, tried to swallow it. In the silence that followed, my words seemed trapped inside the car. They pushed against the windows, our ears, against Mami's voice when she spoke again.

—I know that now. I heard you, before, at that house.

She sobbed into her hands but I did not look at her. Her voice rose in pitch. She said through her fingers, I made up that story because I didn't know the truth was already so bad.

What's weird is that after Mami said that, I finally understood Rudy's lying, that it came from wanting so much to make himself bigger, more significant somehow. In the moment when Mami and I both knew it had to be over, I figured out what he'd needed most from me, what we'd wanted from each other.

I stayed with my parents that night. My dad took me the next week to get my stuff at our apartment while Rudy was at work—as a fireman, a vet tech, a conman, I didn't care anymore. Dad stopped at every fist-sized hole he found hidden behind the picture frames we were taking down. He stooped to look into each one as if he'd find some secret, supporting his weight with a hand on each knee, saying, Sandra, how did this happen? And me shrugging my shoulders, thinking of how Mami had tucked me into my old bed that night, whispering *I'm so sorry*, as if she'd been the one who made the holes.

The only other guy to hit me was you, and only once. I made some joke about your sister. It was a long time ago, back when we just started out, my mom and her faded panic about me never finding someone still a joke between us. We were friends—by then I'd learned to let things grow. This was back before I even met your sister, before you trusted me enough to tell me what your dad had done to her.

We were watching this lame made-for-television special about a driver's ed teacher trying to seduce one of his students. She was only fourteen. I started saying that I thought it was hot. And since you laughed and said I was terrible, I kept going with my weird flirting, saying that I bet you thought it was hot, too.

You even warned me. You said, Don't joke about that, it's not right.

(Of course you didn't know about Victor, about Carl, Rudy. Not yet—not so early on. I was trying to think of them as *my past life*. I didn't know then you'd end up on this list.)

You started biting down hard on nothing. Your fingers dug into your knees with such pressure that the tips of them burned white. There it was—anger fusing with passion. I thought maybe you were about to kiss me, so I whispered, I bet you wish you could get your hand in some fourteen-year-old pussy.

—I told you to shut up, you said.

Blood filled the tops of your ears, turning them red so fast I thought of chameleons, of camouflage. You shifted in your seat and I had the idea you were grabbing a pillow from the couch, but there was nothing in your hand as it charged at me.

Your fist landed by my eye, knocked me off the sofa onto the floor. I looked up at you standing over me, my vision blurred from the hit. The wide square of you wobbled through my watery eyes. It hurt worse than any other time I'd ever been hit. My face grew hot and I could feel a new pulse where the bruise would be.

You turned off the TV and put your face in your hands, and eventually you told me all of it. You explained how it destroyed your mom, how your father had taken his own life just before your mom and sister went to the police. I told myself: he just hit me, but he was defending them; you were a man who would stand up for a woman; you would hit someone else for me. And even though you said, *Oh baby, I'm so sorry, I didn't mean to,* just like Victor and even Rudy at first, the way you couldn't look at me when you said it told me you were different enough, that you meant it. You picked a pillow off the couch and handed it to me, proof of something. I took it as a sign that things would be soft between us, and later, after the whole story, I didn't even want the ice you brought me.

These days, when we wrestle in bed, after you pin me, I joke that I'll tell our hypothetical kids how their dad once punched their mami in the face, splitting open her eye so that she needed twenty stitches, made her blind for two weeks. I tell you I'll need to exaggerate if I want it to really mean anything. And you beg me, every time, not to even play like that.

—What would that make me to them? you say.

I look around our bedroom, my head hanging off the edge of the mattress, at the walls painted your favorite light green, framed pictures of things from our old lives looking back at me, but upside down.

—A monster, I say, head still back. It would make you a monster.

—Exactly, you say.

You pull my head up by the hair and kiss me on the forehead, holding both my hands in one of yours behind my own back, stroking them because it's a reflex by now. You don't smile, or even look at me. You only look off at the pictures that I'm still staring at, and I know you're thinking of the ones we refuse to put up. My scalp aches—the root of every hair wants to scream—but I keep quiet. You squint your eyes at the empty places between the frames, the spots we've taught each other to ignore.

You say, And we both know that monsters don't exist.

I wink. Your lips slip back from your teeth. I say, Pull harder, make me believe you.

Relapsing, Remitting

Javier drove too fast to the university, making them thirty-five minutes early for his wife's first appointment with the new doctor. Across the street from the campus medical complex was a small bakery, and they decided to grab a breakfast of Cuban coffee and toast. So they parked, and Javier walked around to the passenger-side door and Isabel took his arm, pulling on him like a child begging to be picked up. They debated leaving her walker in the trunk, but she decided, because it was a busy intersection, not to risk it.

A bell clinked as Javier held open the bakery's glass door. Two old men sat at the counter, sipping café out of tiny cups. Each of them wore wide-brimmed white hats, and the sun had baked their hands and faces the color of dried palm fronds. They turned on their stools to watch them enter, and each said, a second apart, *Buenas.* Isabel pushed her walker toward one of three round tables—the one furthest into the bakery—while Javier ordered at the counter. Neither of the old men helped her sit; all they could do was look at their hands and clear their throats, but Javier was relieved they'd left her alone.

He sat down across from Isabel a few minutes later, the foam cups of café con leche steaming in his hands, the baskets of toast perched on his arms. The little table rattled each time he placed something down on it.

—What's he gonna make you do? Javier said, his voice hushed.

He blew over the top of his cup. Isabel poured sugar in hers, moving her lips as she counted to ten.

—I don't know. Why would I know that?

She put the sugar down, and the thud shook the table again. She was left-handed, but ever since her entire left side had gone numb three weeks before, she'd done things with her right hand. Javier tapped his spoon on the lip of his cup, then slid it into her coffee for her. Her right hand stirred; the left lay palm up on the table, the fingers curling toward her wrist as if playing an invisible guitar. He rubbed his eyes with the heels of his hands.

—It just seemed like the kind of thing you would know, he said.

—Well I don't, she said.

They looked away from each other and out the window. On the other side of the palm tree–lined street, the University of Miami Medical Complex loomed like an evil factory. The front of it was all glass, tinted a clear sea-green, and they could see four stories of white stone and metal staircases inside, with people running up and down the flights. On the ground floor was a receptionist's desk, and a tall woman sat in a swivel chair behind it, spinning herself from one side to the other. The building looked more like a gym than a place where people conducted research.

Isabel said, I'm pretty sure he won't take any blood.

—Well, thank God for that, Javier said.

He leaned back and patted his barely bulging stomach and smiled at his wife. At the birth of each of their daughters—the most recent one happening just five years earlier—he had not taken his eyes off the curls plastered to her sweaty forehead for fear of seeing blood. And during the week she'd just spent in the hospital, he'd thrown up once after accidentally looking as a nurse changed her IV.

Isabel said she was too nervous to eat and pushed her toast toward him. The butter was spread so thickly that it held her teeth marks from the one bite she'd taken. Still, Javier managed to eat it all.

—What time is Melisa's field trip? she asked.

He chewed the last of the toast and looked at his watch.

—I have to be at the school by nine-thirty, he said. I'll make it—we'll be done here way before then, right? What's her teacher's name again?

Isabel chuckled, the working side of her mouth grinning. The two old men turned their heads to watch her, then went back to their café.

—It's Ms. LeVan, she said. You guys will have fun. Melisa hasn't stopped talking about the Everglades since they studied it in school.

She slumped down further in the chair. She had signed up to go as a chaperone weeks before this first attack. With her right pointer finger, she squashed a bread flake on the table until it crumbled. He reached out and took her hand.

—Come on, he said. Hey, I'll bring you back some mosquitoes.

He stroked her hand, and she rolled her eyes.

—Just as magical as being there, she said.

He forced a laugh, and the old men at the counter must have heard the difference in it, because they didn't turn around as they had before.

The new doctor was fairly certain—ninety-two percent sure, he said when he first met them during Isabel's hospital stay—that what she had was multiple sclerosis. He would need to bring her in for observation to make a concrete decision. He'd need to talk to both of them, get a sense of the case history, he said. Javier made photocopies of every important paper in the house—insurance payments, her birth certificate, both their naturalization papers, documents from every other time Isabel had been treated for anything. Isabel had put the copies in a manila envelope. Javier now had the envelope on his lap, and it sat there throughout the doctor's interview.

On the wall behind the doctor were various framed oversized certificates—one from Cornell, several others from the University of Miami, one from the Multiple Sclerosis Society—and on a shelf, along with some family photographs and a *World's Worst Golfer* mug, was a plastic cross section of a brain, also oversized.

—Let's see you move! the doctor said after fifteen minutes of talking.

He pushed back his chair so quickly that it hit the wall behind him, but the certificates did not rattle at all, as if they'd been super-glued to the wall. He leaned forward, his hands flat on the desk, one on each side of his note-covered legal pad.

Javier and Isabel looked at each other, then back at the doctor, who had a brown poof of hair between two trenches of forehead that reached up and around his head. His eyes were a dull blue but large enough to divert attention from his weak, sunken chin. He was white, clean-shaven, and his smile was too wide. He smoothed down his tie, adjusted his lab coat on his shoulders, and shoved his hands into its vast pockets. Before Javier and Isabel could ask any questions, the doctor came around the desk and said, Come on, come on! Let's not be shy!

He clapped his hands, the sound bouncing off the walls.

In the dimly lit observation room, a dozen or so high-backed swivel chairs sat scattered around a dark wood conference table. The doctor rolled two of the chairs toward the large window, turning one seat toward Javier. Isabel stood on the other side of the window, at the edge of a long padded walkway that ran the length of the room. She held herself up by pushing off two metal railings, one on either side of her. Javier saw her knees cave in toward each other, saw how wisps of dark hair sprawled from the edges of her crotch between her legs, making her thighs look covered in uneven shadows.

—Okay, Isabel, hold those railings and come toward the mirror, the doctor said into a speaker. Just watch yourself and try to relax.

Isabel shut her eyes, then moved. From her white knuckles, her clenched jaw, Javier could see she was suffering, but not from pain. He knew her: had Isabel known that the doctor was going to make her walk in her underwear, she would have prepared. She would have worn underwear that matched her bra, a pair high enough to conceal the broad stretch marks—shiny slashes that covered her stomach like tiger stripes. As it was, she wore a black bra and faded red cotton underpants. When she had taken off her clothes, Javier helping her before retreating to the observation room, he'd seen that she'd put on her underwear inside out, the seams casting off little red threads, the tag wrinkled and washed so many times it was wordless.

—Doctor, Javier said, How come she has to do this in her underwear?

The doctor cocked his head and smiled, and Javier could tell he'd heard this question many times. The doctor removed a pen from the top of his clipboard, clicked it several times, and turned back to the window.

—This is the only way we can make an unhindered observation. Clothes cover what we need to see.

He pointed the pen toward Isabel.

—Watch when she takes this step with her right leg. Do you see how the left hip dips slightly? That shouldn't happen—it's part of what's giving her trouble planting the left leg on time—the hip isn't compensating, it's not lifting back up. That tells us the myelin on the neurons controlling that area has been affected.

Javier watched. He saw the dip.

—That's something clothing would obscure. The damage could have been misinterpreted as *only* in myelin of the neurons controlling the *leg*.

Javier nodded as if he understood. When he swallowed, his throat was dry. He looked down at the clipboard as the doctor scribbled in some sort of code. On a line drawing of a generic woman on the sheet, the doctor circled the left buttock. He'd already circled the entire left leg and the left side of the face.

—Why, Javier said, clearing his throat, Why is it that someone can't be in there with her? He leaned forward in the chair, turning away from the window.

The doctor kept his attention on Isabel as he answered. He said, Actually, we've found that it usually makes patients *more* nervous, and that because they can see the visitor's reaction, they sometimes alter their walk so as to spare the visitor from seeing the extent of their handicap. Which, of course, impacts our observations.

The doctor wrote something on the clipboard without looking down as he wrote it. Turning back to the window, Javier saw that his wife had almost made it halfway across the mat, and that her forehead was glistening.

—Sometimes, the doctor said, patients will keep looking at the visitor, which also impacts their gait. It's one of the reasons we use a one-way mirror rather than a window.

The doctor leaned forward and pushed a black button mounted beneath the glass. He pointed his voice toward the mesh circle next to the button.

—You're doing great, Isabel, really. Keep coming forward.

A moment after the doctor released the button, Isabel bit her bottom lip, sucking the whole thing into her mouth. The doctor clicked his pen shut.

He said to Javier, Also, the mirror helps the patient see what others see. It's a tool for moving away from denial toward acceptance. Facing the truth, so to speak. It can be very beneficial for the patient's mindset in physical therapy.

The doctor stood, tucking the pen into his shirt pocket. He let out a deep sigh and rolled his chair back underneath the table behind them. He patted Javier on the shoulder three times, then squeezed it. Then the hand was gone.

Isabel kept coming. She was so close to the window that Javier could see the chips in the berry-colored polish on her toenails. He saw the loose waves in her thick hair, dark brown and pulled back in a low ponytail, and how she hadn't sprouted even one gray hair yet. When she came a step closer, he could make out the smaller, more subtle stretch marks on the tops of her breasts. He remembered how full they'd been the weeks before their first daughter's birth, how he'd joked that he wanted her to stay pregnant forever if it meant access to breasts like those for the rest of his life. She'd pushed her hand in his face, throwing her head back and laughing, saying, I *hate* you, I *hate* you, while he dotted her neck with kisses.

Javier wanted to look away from the wife staggering toward him, but instead, he stared at the stretch marks, at the faded red underwear, at the bra that didn't match. She looked as if she'd bite through her bottom lip. He forced himself to stare at this pouched face, moonlike from heavy doses of cortisone, sweating, shimmering. He repeated in his head, *This is my wife, this, this,* until the doctor said, Well, come on, Let's go get her dressed.

She should not have any more children. This was the first thing the doctor told them fifteen minutes later, after the nurse had led them from the observation room back into the office. Her lemony perfume had swamped the room and lingered long after she'd shut them in. The doctor sat at the desk, his hands folded on top of it. A new, completely blank notepad waited in front of him, his pen lined up exactly with its top edge.

—Subjecting your body to the stress of pregnancy would be asking too much.

They hadn't planned on any more after the two girls, but Javier had always kept the idea of a third child—the boy—in the back of his throat, waiting to say it out loud once his construction work became steady. He swallowed as the doctor turned to him and recommended a vasectomy.

—Surgery is a lot less of a risk on you than on her.

Javier suddenly felt very aware of his crotch, but the doctor moved on to more comfortable topics. He said chances were good that she'd get better, regaining most motor functions sooner than later. She was young, and her MS was in a phase called relapsing-remitting; this, he explained, was the good phase. She was not as bad off as most MS cases. She would be a good candidate for several experimental medications. He told them this was a disease you could live with, that people don't necessarily die from it. As the doctor went into deeper detail, Javier tried to stop thinking up ways to get out of the vasectomy.

By the time the appointment was over, they each had a stack

of reading material and Isabel had an appointment for what the doctor called a baseline MRI.

—So we can measure future attacks by it.

She began to cry, very softly, when the doctor said this, and he suggested they read the pamphlets about the MS Society and its support groups before looking at any of the other booklets. Javier shifted in his seat, crossed his legs, then took his wife's good hand and squeezed it.

Javier dropped off Isabel at home and, after slapping together sandwiches and throwing them into brown paper bags, he made it to the school in time to see his daughter's class lined up in front of the bus.

—There's my dad, Ms. LeVan! he heard a girl say.

He looked toward the voice and saw his daughter Melisa, stringy and hungry-looking, glaring at him as if he'd refused to show up at all. Then, a dark woman with heavy breasts in a T-shirt reading *Palm Springs North Elementary* jogged toward him. She'd strapped a green-tinted visor to her head, her hair in short black waves that seemed painted on her scalp. Her legs, in knee-length jean shorts, looked too thin to support the weight above them. She shook Javier's hand once she'd come to a stop in front of him.

—Mr. Mendez! So good to finally meet you! I'll put these with the others, she said, grabbing the lunch bags. She had to tug on them twice before he realized he'd been clutching them to his chest.

As they boarded the bus, he asked Melisa if he was supposed to sit next to her. She huffed, *Dad,* and ran down the aisle away from him.

He sat at the front of the school bus near the other chaperones, talking to no one. Someone had already opened the window by his seat, but only when they started driving was there a breeze. He could hear his daughter and the two girls she shared a bench with shrieking near the back of the bus. All the mothers seemed to already know each other, and some had started smearing sunscreen and bug repellant on their arms and legs. Once the bus eased onto the expressway, the teacher turned around to talk to him.

—So, you ever been to Gator Jungle Island?

She had a broad smile, her left canine wrapped in gold.

—I've never even been to the Everglades, he said.

She nodded and smacked her palm against the back of her seat.

—I feel you, she said. You live a place your whole life and never see what you're supposed to while you're there.

He picked at his thumb cuticle until it started to sting.

—That's right, he said.

—Just the way it goes, she said, taking deep breaths and patting her chest as if she'd burped. Then she said, I hope Mrs. Mendez feels better soon.

The note they'd written saying that Javier would take Isabel's place as a chaperone had said only *very ill,* and that she was *so sorry.*

—She's got to be the best homeroom mom I've ever worked with, Ms. LeVan said. Never forgets a kid's birthday, always planning class holiday parties two months early. You know she rounds up more chaperones on her own than when I send letters home with the kids? Your wife—she makes my life easy.

Javier tried to smile. He tried to hear his daughter screaming over the teacher's words. A girl's voice—maybe hers—yelled, *Okay now your turn.*

—I just hope we don't wear her out, the teacher said. I'm praying she volunteers again when your younger one's with me.

—Cristina, he said. Crissy.

—Crissy, right. Cute girls, look like twins. No boys yet? she said, winking.

Javier looked out the window, the palm trees blurring into one solid green-topped streak. He imagined bugs—the wind pushing them against their will—flying through the open window, blinded by the glint of the teacher's gold tooth, smashing into her teeth.

—Not yet, he said. He didn't turn back to face her.

The wind rushing through the bus window had no bugs, but it lifted pieces of his hair off his forehead and made his eyes water. The teacher cleared her throat.

—Well, she said. The less babies you make, the less work for me in the long run, am I right?

They both pretended to laugh, and then the teacher twisted back around, searching for the closest mother.

Gator Jungle Island was not exactly a jungle, and it was definitely not on an island. Javier said this to the group of seven kids he'd been assigned to shepherd around the park, and all of them—even his own daughter—groaned. After a head count, the teacher handed him eight slips of paper—airboat ride tickets, seven children, one adult—and told him a time.

—Y'all are at 1:15. After lunch, just before we leave. See where it is on the map?

She pointed to a colorful laminated brochure, at a picture of what looked like a huge fan sitting in a rowboat. A cartoon alligator wearing a pirate's hat waved from the front of the vessel.

—1:15, there, Javier said. He nodded once.

She winked again and handed him the open map. The corner of her upper lip slid up to reveal the flash of gold, as if the glint were a secret between them.

Javier could not manage to fold the brochure back up, bending every predetermined crease in its opposite direction. By the time he'd warped it into a size that fit his back pocket, his daughter had already led the gang halfway down a mulched path, past a wooden sign, the words *Gator Grabbing—This Way!* etched into it with slashes meant to look like claw marks.

For the majority of the day, he stood back, doing little more than counting every few minutes to make sure there were seven heads, letting his daughter manage the when and where of the group. He honestly did not know where she'd learned to be so bossy, and as he watched her at the front of the V of children—sometimes even walking backwards like a tour guide—he said to himself, *I gotta tell Isabel about this.*

They stroked the tails of baby alligators held by trainers at the Gator Grabbing Grounds. They spent a respectful amount of time examining the dioramas in the Save the Everglades display. They threw handfuls of dirt at the flamingos in Paradise Lagoon until a Gator Guard standing nearby told them to stop. They banged on the glass snake tanks until one of the animals acknowledged them by slightly raising its head and flicking its tongue. Melisa dragged all of them through the ropes course at Survival Swamp, and then, at the Manatee Mania exhibit, they spent half an hour feeding lettuce to what looked to Javier like huge floating turds. By lunch, they'd seen almost everything, and Javier wondered if Melisa had somehow gotten her hands on the park's brochure long before he'd ever seen it.

At 1:00 he managed to take control and reroute the group toward the airboat pavilion. They arrived only three minutes late for their ride. The captain stood at the end of a pier, one leg perched on the rim of a metal boat, waving his arms over his head.

—Welcome folks! he yelled as they walked over the creaking wood.

Melisa, still in front, looked back over her shoulder and said, Be careful, while pointing down to the planks. When she turned back around, Javier added, Right, watch out everyone.

Melisa stopped at the pier's end, and everyone fell in behind her, staggering themselves to get better views of the airboat bobbing on the water. The captain had a long reddish mustache that swooped under his chin. His baseball cap had the word *Junglerrific* embroidered across the front of it.

—Is everybody ready to discover the beauty of the Everglades? he said.

After the children chorused *Yes,* he gave Javier a thumbs-up. From the very back of the group, Javier sent one back. He passed the tickets forward to the captain.

—Sounds like a great group, the captain said as he counted the slips of paper.

Javier looked at the kids, most of them shifting their weight and fidgeting, and he guessed that the captain had given that line to every group he'd ever taken out on the boat.

The captain talked at length about safety, asking if they all knew how to swim or wrestle alligators. He hopped into the airboat and squatted down, then proceeded to grab life vests off the airboat's floor and fling them onto the deck. The kids took several steps back to avoid getting beaned by the neon orange projectiles.

—What's your name, sir? the captain said. Javier looked up from the puddles forming beneath the dripping vests.

—Me? Javier—I mean, Mr. Mendez. I'm her dad.

He pointed to Melisa. She stood with her hands shielding her eyes from the sun, looking only at the captain.

—Okay, Mr. Mendez, you can help me strap these guys in.

He hurled a vest by its black straps, and Javier caught it against his chest, drops of water spraying his face. After standing stunned for a second, he lowered himself onto one knee and began fastening the foam and buckles around the kid closest to him. The boy stuck his arms straight out from his sides and lifted his chin as if about to be launched. Javier clicked the boy's chest straps shut, but the ones around his stomach didn't meet, and so Javier had to turn the boy around and loosen the strap at the buckle. He pulled tight and heard the boy say, *Ouch,* but kept working. Then he heard his daughter say, *No, I can do it,* and when he looked up from the boy he'd been helping, he saw her clicking her vest shut, the captain standing above her with his hands on his hips.

Javier had three more vests to secure when the captain announced that those already wearing one could board the boat.

—Once you're in, he said from his post at the back by the huge fan that would blow them over the Everglades in a few minutes, You sit. No standing. If you're standing you can fall out. Sit down *right away.* Every seat is a good seat. Don't be picky.

Javier turned the recently vested child around toward the boat and pulled the next one closer to him so that he could wrap him in foam. Over the shoulder of the next boy, he saw Melisa stretching her thin leg out over the water.

Thinking he should say something, he yelled, Don't be scared now.

—*Dad,* she said, I'm *not.* She did not turn around when she said this; she focused instead on the small leap she would have to make to get into the boat.

Javier's hand hovered over the next vest as he ignored it to watch her make the jump. She seemed to land fine, but a second after her sneaker thudded against the boat's floor, her head snapped forward and he heard a series of metallic slaps.

—Ah crap, the captain said, rushing over the aluminum benches to get to her.

Javier stood and pushed the squirming kid in front of him out of his way. One of them said, *Uh-oh,* and the others gasped, standing on their toes to see the boat's floor.

Melisa was flat on her stomach on the bottom of the boat, her curly hair flopping over her head and hiding her whole face. She was not crying. In fact, she made no noise at all—she did not say *Dad,* or *Help,* or even *Ouch*—and the only thing Javier thought he heard was the echo of her body hitting the aluminum. He stepped on the edge of the boat to jump in and help her, but all he did was push it away from the dock, making the distance too far to jump.

His daughter did what looked like half a push-up against the floor, lifting her head up enough to look around her. Blood dripped from her chin. Javier thought, *Do not pass out—not now.*

The captain pulled Melisa up by the shoulders and said, You okay sweetie?

She reached up and felt her chin, smearing the blood so that it made a wide blotch over the bottom part of her face. She looked down at her hand, and Javier thought she would definitely cry now. But she just stared at the red-smeared fingers, touching the tips of them to her tongue. He felt himself gag and then swallowed hard to keep from throwing up. The captain held the bottom of his T-shirt to the girl's face, revealing his furry belly to those still on the dock.

—Let the man help you, Javier said.

But she licked her hand and rubbed her chin until red stained her palm and her left cheek like she'd been playing with his wife's makeup. He thought it almost made her prettier—the added color on her face. His stomach started to settle.

—I'm okay, she said. Please—and Javier heard his daughter's voice crack with this—Please, I still wanna go on the boat ride.

He saw her chest heaving, trying to breathe deeply to keep herself from crying like he knew she must have wanted to. She bit her bottom lip, then pressed her hand against her chin, turning around in the boat—away from Javier and the dock, and out of the captain's reach—to face the river of grass surrounding them.

She said, I'm really really okay. Really. She looked at the captain. Can I?

—I'll leave that up to the man in charge, the captain said.

It took a second for Javier to realize that the captain meant him; he'd been watching the drops of blood roll from his daughter's chin, onto her hand, to her wrist, each one gliding toward her elbow. He looked up from the berry-tinted skin to see everyone, even, finally, his daughter, staring at him, waiting to hear his verdict.

The MS Survivors and Families support group met on Thursday nights. Javier had already said he did not see why they needed to go to any meetings, but the night after the field trip, Isabel again brought up that she wanted to go. She waited until after dinner, after their daughter reenacted each minute of the field trip, using the younger daughter as a prop. Isabel kissed her daughter's chin over the patch of gauze, and Javier put them to bed. She now sat at the kitchen counter watching him wash dishes.

—Did Melly eat all of her sandwich at lunch? she said. She said to the countertop, She hasn't been eating.

Javier nodded.

—What did you think of Ms. LeVan? she said.

He barely registered the aching sunburn on the back of his neck. He'd been scrubbing the same dish for close to five minutes.

—You never told me she had a gold tooth, he said.

—I didn't? she shrugged. Well, you can't really see it that much.

Javier placed the dish in the drying rack and picked up the next one off the stack on the counter.

—I guess, he said. It was just weird.

—You spent the day with alligators in the Everglades and you remember a gold tooth, she said. And you think the *teacher* is weird?

—Well you're used to it—to her—the tooth, he said.

He felt like he should talk more to fill the space between them; he had not added one detail to the daughter's story, and Melisa had not asked him to interject. He'd sat pushing his food around with his fork, laughing at all the right places.

—I'm used to Ms. LeVan all right, Isabel said finally. The way that lady takes advantage of me? She practically begged me to be homeroom mom, and I felt bad, you know, I didn't want the kids to suffer. But seriously, one time esa mujer had *me* call up *other* parents to remind them to send some signed permission slip back to school with their kids. I'm sorry, that's the teacher's job. Most parents were like, *Who the hell are you*? on the phone. And that's what I would say, too, if some random mother was calling *my* house instead of the teacher.

Javier smiled as he rinsed the dish and she said, What?

—Prepárate then, he said, because Ms. LeVan already has you down for homeroom mom when she gets Cristina.

—Jesus Christ, Isabel said. That lady, she's trying to destroy me with this homeroom mom shit. I mean, look at me.

Javier kept his eyes on the mounds of soap bubbles filling the sink.

After a long moment, Isabel mentioned the MS support group—weren't the meetings something they could try out for a little while?

Javier rested the just-washed dish back in the sink and said, The doctor told us you would get better with time anyway.

—But I have questions, she said.

—You can do research. Use the computer. Read books. Ask the doctor.

—They're not those kinds of questions, she said. I want to ask *personal* questions. About what happens next. What should we tell the girls—how do I tell Melisa I can't finish out the year as homeroom mom?

His wrinkled fingertips gripped the dishes. The air smelled like burnt rice.

—And other things, she said. I wanna ask if sex will be different.

Javier had moved past frustration weeks ago. He'd almost stopped thinking about it completely. He was surprised, now, that she'd mentioned it outright. But all he let himself do was shrug. He said, Maybe sex'll be better.

He stopped rinsing and faced her. He said, more a joke than anything, We can find out right now.

She laughed—a breathy, deep sound—tired and real. She said, We can play doctor. We can use the walker.

She grabbed it with her good hand and rocked it so that the legs clanked against the floor. She said, Quick, before I don't need it anymore.

It was the first time anything about the walker had been funny.

Something that had been stuck between them broke that moment, he thought, a feeling of uneasiness they'd had while lugging the small metal barricade with them everywhere. Isabel and Javier both looked down as the laugh dissipated. He knew she was waiting for him to say he'd go to the meetings.

He turned back to the sink and said, Today at the field trip, Melisa acted like *she* was the one chaperoning. She bossed the other kids around and hit everything in the park like she had a checklist. Weird, to see her acting like that.

—Sounds right, Isabel said. I should've been there to see it.

She ran the fingers of her good hand up and down the fingers of her bad one.

—Hey, he said. You will, sort of. Cristina's class will take the same field trip, you know that.

—I should have been at both, she said.

He shut off the water. He rolled his head on his neck and felt, all of a sudden, very tired. Isabel tapped and curled her fingers one at a time, an exercise the physical therapist had told them would retrain her brain to control her hand. He looked at the next dinner-crusted plate.

—If you wanna go to those meetings, he said, I'll drop you off and wait in the car. I'll take a crossword puzzle or something.

He turned away from the sink and looked her directly in the face, and he raised his eyebrows, sucked in his lips. He said, It's just, I know—I don't think I could handle those meetings.

Her mouth hung open. Her fingers froze, hovering over the countertop. He knew it would take her a second to remember what they'd been talking about.

—I don't believe this, she finally said.

She grabbed her walker and tried to stand. Javier came around the counter, his hands still wet and soapy from the dishes, and clutched her elbow. He said, Hey—

—Get away from me, she said. Get the fuck away from me.

Her fingers twitched where they gripped the walker's handles. In a normal fight, before the attack, she would have knocked him out of her way. Now she could only refuse to look at him while staggering toward the bedroom. He heard her moving away from him, the four plastic-tipped metal legs tapping the tile as she lifted and pushed, lifted and pushed.

He watched her and her walker make it halfway back to the car where he waited before getting out. Javier tried to hide his rising chest, the released gasp, the snap inside him that meant they'd be okay, as Isabel said two words before he even had a chance to ask about the MS meeting; *Never again.*

Once he shut the walker in the trunk and got back in the front seat, he turned on the engine and looked at her. When she wasn't smiling, he could hardly tell that the left side of her face couldn't hold itself up.

—That bad, huh? he said. Never again?

She said nothing until, after a second, he said, Hello?

She touched his face with her bad hand, pressing her limp fingers against his stubble. When she went to smooth his cheek, she pressed too hard, gently slugging him. She tried to smile, and the droopiness revealed itself, pulling down on her cheek like a scar. She turned toward her window.

—I'm okay, she said. Let's just go get the girls. Please?

He could not tell if she was crying, and so paid extra attention to the road in front of them. They were silent—the radio the only talking they heard—until the car pulled into her parents' driveway.

—Hey, he said, finally looking away from the windshield. He said, Listen.

—It doesn't matter, she said. Forget it. I'm not going anymore anyway.

From the driveway they noticed shadows moving behind the curtains inside the house. He looked down at the big purple flowers on his wife's skirt. He did not know what kind of flowers they were, could not even think of the name of any kind of flower.

—It was too much, she said. That's all. I couldn't decide whether to bust out laughing or kill myself.

Her working hand traced the petals of the flowers printed on her lap. His fingers wrung the hoop of the steering wheel.

—I vote for bust out laughing, he said. At least it's over.

Her hand stopped. She grunted, almost laughed, and without looking at him, she said, Over.

She turned her head side to side as she reached for the door's handle. She opened it as much as she could and said, C'mon, the girls.

He took his own hands off the steering wheel, rested his forehead on the faux wood for just a second, then got out to pull the walker from the trunk. He unfolded the metal legs and pushed the thing close to the seat so she could pull herself out. Once she was up and steadied, he shut her door and walked up the driveway ahead of her.

—Hey, she yelled from behind him. Javier turned back around.

—Watch this, she said.

She cocked her head, let her tongue flop from her mouth. She pressed her bad arm against her chest and pushed the walker along with her good knee, rattling the handles of it with her still-working arm.

She sang, *We can do it, we can walk! Give a listen, we can talk! We are doing what we could not do before.*

Javier knew the song, recognized it even through her exaggerated slurring. It was from a telethon for cerebral palsy that he'd first seen when he was a kid, but it still came on annually. At the end of the telethon, the host parades a group of crippled kids across the stage while flashing the grand total behind them. He remembered seeing it year after year, the same kids coming back with braces on their legs instead of in wheelchairs, then the next year with crutches instead of braces. The host would pull them up front, call them *miracles,* and the grand total would continue to rise. Kids that never got better the host left upstage, the camera avoiding close-ups. Even as a boy, he'd found it impossible to make fun of any of it.

—*We can do it, we can run! We can smile and have fun! And thanks to you, we'll soon do even more.*

Isabel's body convulsed; the lyrics crashed into a breathy squealing noise. She gave up trying to force out the words. She couldn't stop laughing—a laugh that took over and made it hard to breathe, the kind that hurt. She put her bad arm up to her chest again and stuck her tongue back out, trying to stay in character, but she was gone—she swayed behind the walker, her mouth open, her eyes squeezed tight, her face wet and red. She lost her balance and fell on the cement driveway, on her butt. The walker stayed put, sturdy on its four good legs. She was still laughing, harder now, folded over herself.

Javier could not move. He stood planted in the driveway, not sure if he should leave her there, or lift her up, or go tell the girls to stay inside—he did not know which he could make himself do.

She leaned back on her good arm and took a deep breath. She wiped her nose and chin with her left hand, leaving a trail of clear slime from knuckle to wrist. She stared at it as if not knowing what to do. Then, her belly still shaking, she held the hand up as best she could toward her husband, but it barely went above her head.

—Look at my gimpy hand! she said.

She waved her arm from the shoulder and the hand flailed a dead hello. The screen door of the house clapped shut.

—Stop it, Melisa said.

His daughter might have been grinding her teeth, but the swath of gauze covering the bottom of her face hid her clenched jaw. She'd set herself at the edge of the driveway, her hands balled into fists at her side. The younger one stood behind the screen door, her pink palms pressed against the mesh, her face wet as she yelled, Abuela! Melly went outside without permission!

—Melisa, get inside the house, he said. He pointed to the door, to the younger daughter, as he squatted down to help Isabel.

—She can get up by herself, Melisa said.

Isabel coughed, Mellybaby, Dad and me are playing—I was making a joke.

—I don't care, she said. She looked back at her sister and said, *We* don't care. The gauze encased her bottom jaw like thick cobwebs, barely moving as she spoke.

—You heard your father, Isabel said.

The girl did not step forward. All that moved was her head, which swerved from Javier to Isabel on the ground. Her chin jutted forward, like a turtle sunning itself or an egret about to take off. There was a stain of blood showing through the bandage. The younger one yelled, *Melly, come back*! from the doorway, but the daughter ignored her, kept glaring at her mother on the driveway.

—Get up, Melisa said. Get *up* already.

Javier did not let her say any more. He charged toward his

daughter, pulled her off her feet, lifting her by her shoulders. She flailed in his arms. He grunted, *Do not talk to your mother that way. Do you understand*? But she ignored him. She swung her legs into his gut, his ribs, crying loud enough to finally bring the grandmother to the door. He put his hand under her chin, ignoring the gash from the field trip, and pushed her mouth shut. He heard his wife cry out, Javier, *please,* her cut! but he couldn't look at her. His hand tightened around Melisa's jaw.

He said—in her ear, so close he left spit there—You make her feel worse, that's what you do, by telling her to get up. You make her worse.

Between muffled sobs and his daughter's kicks, Javier managed to squeeze his other arm around the girl, pulling her closer to his chest as he sank down to his knees. The youngest daughter wailed from the doorway as the grandmother tried to pull her inside. Isabel yelled, *Hey*! and when he finally faced her, she lifted her arms above her head. The limp one curved down like a dying blade of grass.

—Look, *look,* everybody. I'm fine. I'm *fine.*

Isabel half-smiled, her drooping mouth betraying him as she held up the snapped stalk of her arm. Her hand flopped around like a reptile's severed tail. Tiny rocks littered the driveway and cut into Javier's knees. Melisa pushed the words, *She says she's fine,* through the cage of his fingers, but he only squeezed harder, hoping to strangle the angry animal thrashing at his chest.

Drift

Rebeca led her brother to the canal she'd found two months earlier, a place that before that day she'd resolved never to tell him about. He'd called dibs on the bike they'd stolen from their cousins, so she was on foot. He rode next to her, standing on the pedals and circling around her as she jogged toward the canal. When he saw the dust kicked up by the tires settling on his clean sneakers, Jovany said, This better be good.

The canal ran underneath an overpass that the city had abandoned and left unconnected to the main expressway, so the spot was quiet despite being surrounded by an exploding Miami. Steep dirt slopes led down to the water, and tall weeds spiked all along the banks. This canal wasn't close to any houses—they'd been living with their uncle Juanfe and his family for almost two months before Rebeca had even found it.

Once she could see the rusted guardrail, Rebeca started counting, in her head, the number of palm trees she'd used to mark the spot along the canal—six down from the overpass—where less than half an hour earlier she'd found the dead body.

Rebeca ran up to the rusty part of the rail and pointed into the water.

—Look, she said.

Jovany came up behind her. The body was so close to the water's edge that it looked as if it were resting its head on the shore. He was still face down. She'd guessed it was a man because of the short hair. He wore jean overalls that had dark brown smears between the legs. These canals had no current—they were oily and silent enough for mosquitoes to walk on them—but one of the dead man's arms fanned away from him, away from where Rebeca stood next to Jovany. She crossed her arms over her chest, determined not to hold her brother's hand.

Jovany said, Oh my God. She could not read his look—if he was happy or scared. Ever since he'd started at Edison Junior High and left her behind in the fifth grade at their old school, she'd had trouble interpreting his smile. He jumped over the guardrail.

—I saw it today after school, she said. I wanted to wait for you, before I got closer.

She had pedaled harder than she thought possible on the bike ride back to grab Jovany. She'd found him in their cousin Rosario's bedroom, the one Juanfe had declared theirs until their mom came back. She'd stood with her hands gripping the doorframe, watching her brother unlace the pair of sneakers their mom had given him before leaving to go after their father. Jovany had been so focused on the shoes that he jumped when she finally said, *I found something.*

Her hands still ached from gripping the bike's handles, and she felt a blister budding on her thumb. She stepped over the guardrail toward Jovany. She swallowed, her throat rough from running beside him.

—Oh my God, he said again, softly this time. You're not scared?

She wrinkled her face at him, trying to look mad that he'd even asked.

—*No,* she said.

As they started down the steep sides of the canal, dirt and small rocks rolled into the water. *Careful,* he mumbled. She held out her hand to him, but he grabbed her by the wrist.

Now that they were closer, the air smelled something like mildew and spoiled food. Rebeca covered her nose and mouth with her hand. Jovany went ahead of her and said, It's not *that* bad. She dropped her hand from her nose and put the inside bottom of her thumb in her mouth so that she could suck on the blister. The skin tasted salty.

—Should we tell somebody? she said.

Jovany looked up to where they had left the bike, then he looked at his sister, squinting. She felt her face getting hot, so she looked down at his sneakers. Their mother had left almost four months ago, but Jovany cleaned them so often they still looked new. But now, she saw him kick the dirt. He said, Who would we even tell?

Rebeca didn't know if she was supposed to answer him, or what her answer would even be. To share the secret with any of their cousins meant getting in more trouble, and Tío Juanfe had told them too many times to stay on his wife Cacha's good side. Besides, no one had been at Juanfe's house other than Jovany. All three cousins, Rosario—the oldest at fourteen, older than Jovany by a year—Teresa, and Gabriel, went to Immaculate Conception, a Catholic private school that let out later than the county elementary and junior high. Juanfe always picked them up, and Cacha had had to start working night shifts at the hospital on top of her regular ones.

Jovany took two long steps and picked up a dried palm frond, then got closer to the body. Rebeca followed him.

—Don't touch it, she said. It could have diseases.

—I'm not stupid, Jovany said.

He poked the body with the big dry leaf. He squatted down near the head; the face was turned toward the water. He sniffed the air and cleared his throat. When he turned back to Rebeca, his smile was so big she took a step back.

—I don't think he's been here that long, there's no bugs, he said.

She kept her hand in her mouth, the salt taste mingled now with blood.

Jovany looked at the head even closer, squatting down so low that his butt almost touched the dirt. He lifted the head by the hair, and she heard water trickle, but he stood between her and the face, so she couldn't see.

—Come look at this, he said, his free hand waving her over.

She crossed her fingers behind her back, then squeezed her nose shut with her other hand and squatted beside him. He was still holding the head up by the hair.

The man's face looked almost human. Everything was where it was supposed to be, but his lips, cheeks, and nose were very swollen, and there were purple splotches on his cheeks and forehead. The eyelids were almost all black.

—He musta closed his eyes before he died I bet, Jovany said.

Jovany reached out to touch the face, but Rebeca grabbed his arm and yanked it toward her. Stop it, he said, pulling his hand from hers, but he didn't try to touch the face again. He lowered the head back into the water. They sat there silent, staring. Rebeca realized she'd uncrossed her fingers when she'd gone for her brother's hand, but since nothing bad had happened as a result, she didn't re-cross them. Jovany pulled his T-shirt collar over his nose.

—He looks like a cartoon, Rebeca said finally. She watched her brother to see if he would laugh at the funny voice that pinching her nose gave her.

—I bet he maybe killed himself, he said. He turned toward her, and though she couldn't see his mouth, she knew from the crinkling skin around his eyes that he was smiling.

—What should we do now? she said.

Jovany looked back up to the bike, then up and down the length of the canal. It was perfectly straight for as far as they could see. He turned his head, looking at the overpass for a long time. Rebeca watched him, waited for him to say something, then finally turned to her blister, the bubble of it shining like a red gem.

—This is a cool place, huh? she said. She dug the thumb with the blister into the dry soil.

She had never known if there were many canals around the apartment complex they used to live in, because when their dad still lived there, he had never allowed them to go far from their block. Even after he left for the last time, and their mom had gotten to the point where she was more worried about tracking him down than anything else, they never went past the street corners he'd set up as boundaries. It wasn't until a couple weeks into living at Juanfe's house that his wife Cacha had pushed them to play outside, anywhere in the neighborhood, away from her kids and her house.

—It's quiet, he finally said. He pulled up a clump of dry grass and let it fall from his fingers. We should get him out of the sun.

He stood, wiped his hands on his shorts. Help me out, he said.

Jovany found another palm frond up near the bike, and he pushed the man all the way in the water again with his shoe. They used the fronds to guide the floating man toward the shade a few yards away. Jovany kept the man close to the shore. His palm frond was bigger and went deeper into the water, and he was in the front. Rebeca used hers to keep the man's legs from spreading too far apart. When they started moving the man, she put her shirt over her nose just as Jovany had done.

The air was much cooler under the overpass. After they'd slid the man into the shade, Jovany jogged a little ways away from the body, lowered his shirt back down, and coughed, but Rebeca stayed near the body, close to the water, in case he started to float away.

—It's not *that* bad, she said this time, making fun of him.

—Very funny, Rebekita.

This was what both their parents had always called her. Their father called Jovany *Joey.* Their mother had hated that. The smaller fights between them would start with her mother yelling things like, *That's not what I named him,* to point out who had and hadn't been around to decide something like a name. Tío Juanfe and Cacha never used any nicknames for them; Rebeca hadn't heard *Rebekita* in almost four months.

—Don't ever call me that, she said softly. Don't ever again.

Jovany came back into the shade and put one hand on each of her shoulders. He hugged her to him, and his underarms smelled like grown man.

—Hey, hey, he said. Cacha is wrong, okay? Mom's coming back. You're still Rebekita. So relax.

Rebeca did not want to say that after so many months she was starting to believe her aunt more than her brother, so she said nothing. He let go of her shoulders and looked at the man in the water.

—Cacha's a bitch anyways, he said. Don't tell on me that I said that.

He cleared his throat, stood up straighter, and said to the water, Don't believe anything people won't say to your face.

Rebeca said, Yeah, because she didn't know what he wanted her to say, and because she wanted him to think she understood everything he ever talked about. Their arms touched while they stared at the man in the water.

—I want you to go stand over there, Jovany said, moving away from her. He pointed to the place they had just stood. I'm gonna drag him out.

She wanted to tell him no, that he should just leave it, but before she could, Jovany pulled the shirt back over his nose, covering the bottom of his face. His eyebrows were very dark. She didn't like how scary they looked—drifting alone above the white cotton—so she left her brother in the shade and walked back into the sun like he'd ordered. By the time she turned back around, Jovany had positioned himself above the man, ready to do the job alone. She lowered her shirt from her nose.

It didn't take a long time to move him, but it looked hard. Jovany pulled with both hands on one side of the man's overalls, then used both hands to pull the other side level, alternating each pull so that the man got dragged up in a zigzag. Jovany wiped his head with his forearm, and Rebeca was relieved that she didn't have to remind him about diseases.

He stopped pulling once the dead man was only in the canal from the knees down. The water made soft lapping sounds around the clothes. She could hear her brother's hard breathing. He had his back to her.

—Come on, he said.

He looked to his left, up at the overpass support columns, at the dark shadows between them. He spit in that direction, but a string of saliva clung to his chin, and he quickly wiped it off with his arm. Rebeca said from her spot in the sun, Gross.

—Come *on*, he said again. He turned to face her. Help me flip him.

She walked closer to them, blinking as she came into the shade.

—Really? she said. You really wanna flip him?

—I thought you weren't scared.

He held his hands out and lunged a step toward her, trying to touch her. She darted to the side and they both laughed when she said, Stop it, Jovany! They faced the body. Grooves in the dirt around him showed the dragging.

—I'm *not* scared, she said. She looked at their feet. Jovany's sneakers were very dirty now, especially at the toes where they had sunk into the mud. Her own shoes were still mostly white—just a little dusty from the run to the canal—and she wanted to wipe them off. I just don't want to get dirty, she said.

Jovany looked at her looking at his sneakers.

—Too late for that, he said.

She didn't touch the man's skin. Instead, she pulled and pushed him by his clothes. When he finally flopped over, one of his legs splashed back in the canal, but she stood on the other side of him, so only Jovany got wet. When they finished, Jovany bent forward with his hands on his knees, breathing hard. The dead man's stomach pushed out the pockets on the front of the overalls as far as they'd go, pulling tight on the straps at his shoulders. Just like a cartoon, she thought.

—He didn't look so fat in the water, she said.

—He smells worse now, too, he said.

Rebeca didn't think it was that much worse, but she didn't say anything.

—We can't tell Juanfe, Jovany said. He'll think something bad.

—And especially not Tía Cacha, she said.

Jovany glared at her. He bit his lower lip and wrinkled his forehead. He looked exactly like their father when angry, and since she'd never noticed this before just then, she stepped back.

—Why would we ever tell Cacha *anything*? he said.

Rebeca's mouth opened a little, then it closed. She had learned never to talk back to adults, and her brother's face confused her, so she took too long to say, What's your problem? Jovany turned and marched up to the bike, kicking dirt behind him with each hard step. Rebeca stood there, glancing back at the dead man. His mouth looked so much like a smile that she almost smiled back, until she saw that Jovany had left her alone. She got to the top of the canal and was surprised to see him still there, sitting next to the bike. He stuck his chin out at it and said, You take it. I don't want to give the bike diseases.

As they walked back to Juanfe's house, Rebeca pushed the bike home instead of riding it so that Jovany could keep up, the handlebar rubbing against her blister the whole way.

Their cousins were at the dining room table doing homework when they got back. Gabriel's assignment was to color a drawing of Mary holding baby Jesus, so there were crayons sprawled all over his end of the table.

—Where were *you*? Rosario said without looking up.

Her brown hair was so long that she always bragged about sitting on the ends of it by accident. Jovany had asked once if that happened to her on the toilet, too.

—None of your business, Jovany said.

—Dad! Rosario said. Rebeca came up to the table and saw that Rosario had drawn a string of zeros on the lined paper in front of her. Rosario did not look at Rebeca, but she stretched her arm over the writing to hide it.

Jovany mumbled something behind her and escaped to Rosario's room before Juanfe could come out from the kitchen.

Juanfe stood in the doorway of the dining room. He had a close-cut beard and wore the same pants—with paint splatters on them, all sorts of colors—that she'd seen him wearing back when he had a job and left the house at the same time as Cacha. Juanfe still installed air conditioners for people sometimes, or fixed refrigerators in the neighborhood for cash, and when he did, he would tell stories about the insides of other people's houses to all five of them while they ate. Juanfe always cooked dinner wearing those pants—he called them his Work Pants—because he said it was hard work, cooking for five whining kids.

He was wiping his hands on a towel. What is it *now*, he said.

Rosario pointed at Rebeca and said, She won't tell me where she was.

—She doesn't *have* to tell you, he said.

—And Jovany said something bad to me, I heard him, Rosario said.

Gabriel and Teresa looked up at their father. Rebeca heard Gabriel kicking the table leg with his feet.

—Rosario, please, I didn't hear anything. You need to stop this. You're too old.

He threw the towel over his shoulder and put his hand on the back of Rosario's chair. The girl covered up the zeros even more, but she kept writing them, the pencil moving in bigger and bigger circles. She said to Rebeca, Your mom didn't call today either.

—Rosario, enough, Juanfe said.

—She *never* will. And you'll be homeless when my mom kicks you out, she said.

Juanfe grabbed her by the back of the arm, pinching her with his huge hands, and said, *Ya te lo dijo bastante veces* through gritted teeth. He pulled her from the chair into the kitchen, and she screamed, but Rebeca couldn't hear what Juanfe whispered as he hit her. Teresa and Gabriel looked at each other, and Teresa covered her mouth because she started to laugh. Rebeca looked at Jovany's shut door, then at her cousins, who were now staring at her. She leaned forward across the table.

—*Your* mamá is a bitch, Rebeca whispered, though she didn't need to, because Juanfe would not have heard her over Rosario's wailing.

Rebeca ran, weaving through the living room furniture, and grabbed the doorknob to Rosario's room, opened it, and slammed it shut behind her. Jovany was sitting on the bed, his shoes still on. He looked confused. She pressed her back to the door and stood with her weight against it for a few minutes, long after she heard Teresa and Gabriel yell *Daaaaad* in unison. Juanfe never came and knocked. They knew he had run out of excuses—for them, for his own kids, and for his sister—and when he yelled thirty minutes later that dinner was ready, Rebeca and Jovany ate while watching television—something their cousins were never allowed to do.

During an especially loud commercial, she whispered to Jovany, What if they find out?

He finished chewing, then whispered back, They won't. Only you and me know, nobody else. Stop talking about it already.

He sounded angry with her, but then he gave her a wide smile. A big black bean stuck to one of his bottom front teeth, making it look like it was missing, but she didn't tell him. She didn't want to ruin the secret, so she smiled back. And she ate all of her food even though Juanfe had burned the rice again.

The next day, Rebeca sat at her desk, kicking her legs more than usual, anxious for school to be over. Even though she was in fifth grade, she in no way felt she ruled the school the way the other fifth graders thought they did. She knew there was a sixth grade somewhere, in another school, and that being in it was inevitable—it had happened to Jovany, and she was next.

When she'd first found the canal, it had helped school go by faster for her. During class, she would think about where around the canal she could find good rocks to throw to make the biggest splash, or she imagined herself crouched down and staring at any bugs floating by the water's edge. But by the end of that day's language arts class, just before lunch, she knew she wanted to talk to the dead man, and since she'd settled on it so early, all she could do was pick at her blister and wait.

She did not stay to get her math test back at the end of the day. She didn't care how she'd done, or whether she'd have to get Jovany to sign their dad's signature to it again. Everyone else swarmed the teacher to get their grade, but she ran from the room.

The bike was in the backyard, leaning against the chain-link fence. When she got closer to it, she saw a note taped to the handlebars. It was in Rosario's handwriting, and it said, *This is ours. You can't use it anymore.* Rebeca left the note on the bike so that Jovany would find it when he got home. Together, she thought as she ran to the canal, together they'd figure out how to get Rosario into worse trouble with Juanfe.

She could smell the dead man from the top of the canal—like wet wood, like swamp and something too sweet. But it was quiet the way it was always quiet there, the cars on the expressway far off, behind her, and no one around.

He was where they had left him, and he still looked very fat underneath his overalls around his belly, but Rebeca thought he looked sunken around his shoulders, like he was sad, as though someone had just told him bad news. She approached him slowly and sat below him on the slope of the canal's edge, so that she was right near the water: far from his face, but close to his knees. The water was absolutely still.

She looked at his face for a long time without saying anything. She crawled up closer on her hands and knees next to him in the dirt. The patches on the forehead, nose, and chin were the same yellowish green as the hunks of spit left on sidewalks by boys walking to school in the mornings ahead of her. She waved away a fly that was poking in his nostril. She cocked her head at the yellow patch on his forehead and said out loud, Ouch.

She said to him, I wonder what happened to you. The fly settled on his chest and crawled underneath his shirt. She kept breathing through her mouth but her eyes watered. She blew another fly away from his cheek. There were dry cracks in his lips, but his mouth was still swollen and smiling.

—Even you can smile, she said, lowering her face to look closely at his mouth. You even died and you're still happy.

She felt cold all over for just a second, and she worried that maybe she had to pee. She moved to bend over his face so that it was directly under hers. No part of her touched him, and her arms strained to keep herself hovering above his mouth.

—Hey, she whispered. She heard a buzz near her ear.

Then she yelled it—Hey!—without moving. Her voice echoed underneath the overpass. She yelled more things, there close to his face. Stop smiling, stop it! She waited and heard the echo again. Stupid, she yelled. Stupid man! Hey, what's wrong with you? She laughed at how her voice moved around the two of them.

She bent her neck back to look up at the concrete beams running from one side of the canal to the other, put there to support the forgotten overpass. There was no graffiti, and the concrete looked smooth.

—Hey, she said, then listened. She yelled random sounds: woot, la-la-la, nuh-uh. She kept looking at the beams as if she would see the sound bounce above her. She tilted her head so far back while kneeling that she felt the skin on her neck stretch and felt dizzy. With her head all the way back she said, Rebeca. She closed her eyes and shouted, Rebekita.

She imagined that word being the one to wake the man up, make him open his purple-lidded eyes, thrust his rotten hand toward her wide-open neck. She looked down at him quickly, as if she'd catch him peeking at her. She said, Go, do it. She hovered so close to his face that she couldn't see anything clearly, just amazing colors around his mouth, the hues almost enough to keep her close to him had it not been for the smell. She couldn't pretend anymore—that smell was killing her.

She moved away and leaned back on her hands, and said, See?

After a few minutes, she pulled her knees up to her chin and felt their soft hairs against her lips. Then she hugged her legs and considered telling him the things she couldn't talk about with anyone else, especially not Jovany. She could tell him what Jovany had said not to think about: how their mom had chased the car of one of their dad's friends—screaming down the street in front of the whole complex and then sitting in the road until cars honked—after he had given her their dad's message: that he wasn't coming back at all. He'd gone back to his mother in Cuba—where she still lived—because after two kids and so many jobs, he'd just been happier there. Rebeca watched from the living room, how her mother hit the man over and over again with her purse and then with her fists until the man said, *Fuck this,* and ran out of the door. She could tell the dead man how their mom had screamed, *This man will be the end of me* while driving them to Juanfe's to spend the week, and how even though she'd never seen her mom so angry and sad at the same time, she never thought that what she meant by *the end* was that *she* wouldn't come back for them either.

She felt that same cold from before come over her again when she heard voices behind her. She jerked up and listened, and knew that there were several of them. She had never, in her two months of going there, ever seen anyone else at the canal. She looked at the man's body and wanted to hide him from whoever was coming, and that's when she first thought that she could get in trouble because of him. She looked where the voices were coming from at the canal's edge, then back at the man, and she ran up the side of the canal to the dark places between the overpass supports to hide in the shadows.

She squatted behind the small cement barrier and was surprised it almost completely hid her; the pits between the columns were deeper than she'd guessed.

A boy's voice yelled, Holy shit, man! A moment later she could see him. He had on baggy basketball shorts.

Another boy said, How can you stand that smell, man?

—Cuz it smells like your mom, the boy with the shorts said, not turning away from the body. She heard other boys laugh at this, their voices ricocheting underneath the overpass, but Rebeca thought what he'd said was stupid.

A third voice said, Don't touch it, and she knew that Jovany was there.

—This is so cool! the second boy said.

Rebeca could see Jovany and the three other boys near the water. Her brother walked up and stood at the man's head, turning his back to her hiding place. All the boys were looking down at the body.

Jovany said, Told you. He looked around, past the boys. I found it here yesterday.

Rebeca's mouth dropped open.

—Does anybody know? You tell anyone? the boy with the shorts said. He spit into the water. Jovany dug his toe into the dirt. His sneakers were filthy.

—Nah. Nobody else knows. Just you guys.

Rebeca bit her bottom lip to keep from saying something.

—This guy is nasty, one of them said. Shorts boy backed away a little and started coughing. The boy closest to the body leaned down and ran his hands over the leg pockets.

—Nothing, he said.

He walked over next to Jovany and bent down again. Check this out, he said. He grabbed a fistful of the man's hair and lifted the head and shoulders off the ground, then let it fall with a sick thump. One boy said, *Whoa*, another said, *Shit*.

—Come, on. Don't mess with him, man, Jovany said. He shoved the boy, but Rebeca saw her brother was smiling. The other boy grabbed the hair again and shook the head side to side. He said in a high voice, Oh don't hurt me! and all the friends laughed, even Jovany.

Rebeca wished the man would wake up now and choke them all.

Jovany bent down near the man's face. She watched him slowly put his hand near the face and pull open an eyelid, even after one of the other boys said, *Don't do it, man.* All three of the other boys stood behind him and watched him peel it back. Two had their T-shirts over their noses. They made gagging sounds, but Rebeca could not see what Jovany had shown them under the lid. She blinked hard, her eyes blurred from tears.

Jovany stayed crouched next to the man's face and got closer. He stared at the man's mouth. One of the boys said, *What?*

—Nothing, Jovany said. He just. He's, like, smiling.

The boys all looked at the mouth and were quiet for a second.

—Maybe he likes you, Shorts boy said. The other boys laughed.

—Maybe you should kiss him, another boy said.

Jovany stood up and was laughing, too, but not as hard.

—Shut up, he said. He scratched the back of his head the way Rebeca knew he always did when he was embarrassed.

—Maybe he wants to be your new dad, Shorts boy said. Rebeca saw that Shorts boy had crooked teeth and that he barely had a mustache.

—Or your new mom! he added. They all bent over laughing, even Jovany, whose laughs were big and bouncing off the concrete.

Jovany finally said, Good one. He looked for a long time up and down the length of the canal, squinting hard, and then he took a big breath. He bent back over the body.

—Hey Dad, he said.

The boys were cracking up. Rebeca balled up her fists. Her legs started to burn from crouching for so long.

Jovany said, Man, Dad. You are the ugliest dad.

The boys covered their mouths with their hands, still laughing. Another voice said, For real, man. Jovany kept giggling as he talked to the body. Rebeca thought he looked crazy. He squatted back down next to him again.

—I want to tell you about my day at school. He held in a laugh, then finished, But you're so fucking ugly that I can't stand to look at you, Dad.

The echoes made it sound like a hundred people laughing. Her brother's was the meanest one, and Rebeca thought for sure it was the loudest.

Jovany pulled back his arm and slapped the dead man's face. Brown liquid shot out of the mouth toward the boy standing on the other side of the head.

—Nasty, he screamed. He pushed the head with his foot. It looked like he'd kicked it.

Rebeca took off running behind the columns, climbing over the concrete barrier once she was out of columns to hide behind. When she got to the top of the canal, she saw that Jovany's friends had bikes. She ran past them, all the way home, thinking about how scary her brother had looked while hitting the face.

Juanfe held the van's sliding door open, and the last kid, Gabriel, climbed down from among his dad's old tools. When Juanfe saw Rebeca running so hard and crying, he yelled to Rosario, Go in the house, and jogged to meet her in the street.

—Who hurt you? He put his hands on her shoulders.

—Tío, she said. She was breathing so hard that it hurt, and she had a bad pain in her side, but the air smelled so much better away from the canal. She collapsed on the sidewalk, crying so hard it sounded like hiccups. She pushed her hand into the side that ached. He bent down next to her and waited.

—Tío, somebody's dead.

Her uncle's eyes shot open more than she'd ever seen. He squeezed her arms so hard she winced.

—And Jovany—but she couldn't finish.

He picked her up and carried her to the van, put her in the passenger seat, ran fast to the door of the house and yelled something inside, locked it behind him, and jumped in the van. The keys jangled in his trembling hands, but he eventually started the engine.

They had already backed out of the driveway when he said, Tell me where to go.

She said, The canal. By the overpass, the empty one.

When she realized he knew exactly how to get there, and that the drive took just minutes, she was mad at herself for ever thinking she had found something special.

Juanfe drove over the tall grass up to the palm trees.

—Where, he said.

She pointed to the overpass through the windshield.

—There, by the water.

He flung open the door and jumped from the van without shutting it off. With the door open, Rebeca could hear laughing, all the way up there on the banks, and she knew that things had gotten worse. She climbed down from the van and took off after her uncle, who was already yelling something as he went down the steep side of the canal. The three other boys ran out from under the overpass, but Jovany was not with them. Rebeca passed them, and they were quiet as they watched her run by.

One of them said, Is that his sister? Does he got a sister?

Before Rebeca could see them, she heard Juanfe say, What the fuck is going on here, and she heard smacking sounds. What the fuck is wrong with you?

Juanfe almost never cursed. She ran under the overpass and saw Jovany on the ground, huddled with his hands over his head to protect himself. His eyes were closed.

Juanfe was beating him, throwing his fists into every part of Jovany's body. When Jovany sank lower to the ground, Juanfe picked him up by his shirt, but then threw him back down into the dirt. Then Juanfe looked at the body and gagged, burping into his hand. Jovany tried to stand, but Juanfe grabbed his whole face with his free hand and shoved him back down.

—You are sick, Juanfe said.

—Tío, please, Jovany said. Tears left clean streaks on his dusty face. Rebeca stood on her toes and moved closer to the body.

The dead man looked terrible. Somehow he wasn't fat anymore; his overalls were baggy around his stomach. A purple-brown liquid, like motor oil, spilled from the side of him. Angry flies swarmed all over the puddle. His mouth hung open, and someone had pulled the black tongue out very far—it looked like something he could choke on. She had guessed his teeth were crooked and was confused to finally see that they were straight, but that all the ones on the sides were completely missing, leaving big black holes in his smile.

—Leave now, Rebeca, Juanfe said.

That's when Jovany saw that she was there.

—Wait, her brother said. His voice was quiet but Juanfe slapped him with the back of his hand. Even after the slap, Jovany said, Rebeca, please, tell him—

—Get back in the van! Juanfe yelled at her, but he started to cough.

She didn't move. She didn't know what to say. Juanfe looked quickly at the body and said, Holy Mother of Christ, and crossed himself over and over again until he started to gag. He stumbled to the columns and finally vomited in the shadows between them.

Kneeling down with his back to the three of them, Juanfe covered his face with his hands. He cried into them, chanting softly, My fucking sister, my fucking sister.

She knew Jovany heard him—the words grew larger off every column, with every echo—because he dropped his head to his sneakers. A crust of mud caked them completely. Flies circled his feet, and when they landed on the laces, he did not kick them away. Jovany's glare rested on the shoes for too long. She waited for her brother to slap the air, to crush each fly's veiny wings, but he refused to move, refused to protect his more-than-ruined shoes. A dull ache pulsed up her thumb toward her palm, and when she looked down at her hand, she saw that the blister had burst, the yolk of it dripping down in a lonely bead. Tattered flakes of skin rimmed the raw part, and the very center glowed a rotten purple. She hid it behind her back and cradled it in her other hand, squeezing her fingers together so hard it caused a new ache, one big enough to keep the blister's sting a secret.

How to Leave Hialeah

It is impossible to leave without an excuse—something must push you out, at least at first. You won't go otherwise; you are happy, the weather is bright, and you have a car. It has a sunroof (which you call a moonroof—you're so quirky) and a thunderous muffler. After fifteen years of trial and error, you have finally arranged your bedroom furniture in a way that you and your father can agree on. You have a locker you can reach at Miami High. With so much going right, it is only when you're driven out like a fly waved through a window that you'll be outside long enough to realize that, barring the occasional hurricane, you won't die.

The most reliable (and admittedly, the least empowering) way to excuse yourself from Hialeah is to date Michael Cardenas Junior. He lives two houses away from you and is very handsome and smart enough to feed himself and take you on dates. Your mother will love him because he plans to marry you in three years when you turn eighteen. He is nineteen. He also goes to Miami High, where he is very popular because he plays football and makes fun of reading. You are not so cool: you have a few friends, but all their last names start with the same letter as yours because, since first grade, your teachers have used the alphabet to assign your seats. Your friends have parents just like yours, and your moms are always hoping another mother comes along as a chaperone when you all go to the movies on Saturday nights because then they can compare their husbands' demands—*put my socks on for me before I get out of bed, I hate cold floors,* or, *you have to make me my lunch because only your sandwiches taste good to me*—and laugh at how much they are like babies. Michael does not like your friends, but this is normal and to be expected since your friends occasionally use polysyllabic words. Michael will repeatedly try to have sex with you because you are a virgin and somewhat Catholic and he knows if you sleep together, you'll feel too guilty to ever leave him. Sex will be tempting because your best friend Carla is dating Michael's best friend Frankie, and Michael will swear on his father's grave that they're doing it. But you must hold out—you must push him off when he surprises you on your eight-month anniversary with a room at The Executive Inn by the airport and he has sprung for an entire five hours—because only then will he break up with you. This must happen, because even though you will get back together and break up two more times, it is during those broken-up weeks that you do things like research out-of-state colleges and sign up for community college classes at night to distract you from how pissed you are. This has the side effect of boosting your GPA.

During these same break-up weeks, Michael will use his fake ID to buy beer and hang out with Frankie, who, at the advice of an ex-girlfriend he slept with twice who's now living in Tallahassee, has applied to Florida State. They will talk about college girls, who they heard have sex with you without crying for two hours afterward. Michael, because he is not in your backyard playing catch with your little brother while your mother encourages you to swoon from the kitchen window, has time to fill out an application on a whim. And lo and behold, because it is October, and because FSU has rolling admissions and various guarantees of acceptance for Florida residents who can sign their names, he is suddenly college bound.

When you get back together and he tells you he's leaving at the end of June (his admission being conditional, requiring a summer term before his freshman year), tell your mom about his impending departure, how you will miss him *so* much, how you wish you could make him stay just a year longer so you could go to college at the same time. A week later, sit through your mother's vague sex talk, which your father has forced her to give you. She may rent *The Miracle of Life*; she may not. Either way, do not let on that you know more than she does thanks to public school and health class.

—I was a virgin until my wedding night, she says.

Believe her. Ask if your dad was a virgin, too. Know exactly what she means when she says, Sort of. Try not to picture your father as a teenager, on top of some girl doing what you and Carla call a Temporary Penis Occupation. Assure yourself that TPOs are not sex, not really, because TPOs happen mostly by accident, without you wanting them to, and without any actual movement on your part. Do not ask about butt-sex, even though Michael has presented this as an option to let you keep your semi-virginity. Your mother will mention it briefly on her own, saying, For that men have prostitutes. Her words are enough to convince you never to try it.

Allow Michael to end things after attempting a long-distance relationship for three months. The distance has not been hard: you inherited his friends from last year who were juniors with you, and he drives down to Hialeah every weekend to see you and his mother and Frankie. Still, you're stubborn about the sex thing, and still, you can't think of your butt as anything other than an out-hole. Michael has no choice but to admit you're unreasonable and dump you.

Cry because you're genuinely hurt—you *love* him, you *do*—and because you did not apply early-decision to any colleges because you hadn't yet decided if you should follow him to FSU. When the misery melts to fury, send off the already-complete applications you'd torn from the glossy brochures stashed under your mattress and begin formulating arguments that will convince your parents to let you move far away from the city where every relative you have that's not in Cuba has lived since flying or floating into Miami; you will sell your car, you will eat cat food to save money, you are their American Dream. Get their blessing to go to the one school that accepts you by promising to come back and live down the street from them forever. Be sure to cross your fingers behind your back while making this promise, otherwise you risk being struck by lightning.

Once away at school, refuse to admit you are homesick. Pretend you are happy in your tiny dorm room with your roommate from Long Island. She has a Jeep Cherokee and you need groceries, and you have never seen snow and are nervous about walking a mile to the grocery store and back. Ask the RA what time the dorm closes for the night and try to play it off as a joke when she starts laughing. Do not tell anyone your father never finished high school. Admit to no one that you left Hialeah in large part to piss off a boy whose last name you will not remember in ten years.

Enroll in English classes because you want to meet white guys who wear V-neck sweaters and have never played football for fear of concussions. Sit behind them in lecture but decide early on that they're too distracting. You must do very well in your classes; emails from the school's Office of Diversity have emphasized that you are special, that you may feel like you're not cut out for this, that you should take advantage of the free tutors offered to students like you. You are important to our university community, they say. You are part of our commitment to diversity. Call your mother crying and tell her you don't fit in, and feel surprisingly better when she says, Just come home. Book a five-hundred-dollar flight to Miami for winter break.

Count down the days left until Noche Buena. Minutes after you walk off the plane, call all your old friends and tell them you're back and to get permission from their moms to stay out later than usual. Go to the beach even though it's sixty degrees and the water is freezing and full of Canadians. Laugh as your friends don their back-of-the-closet sweaters on New Year's while you're perfectly fine in a halter top. New England winters have made you tough, you think. You have earned scores of ninety or higher on every final exam. You have had sex with one and a half guys (counting TPOs) and yes, there'd been guilt, but God did not strike you dead. Ignore Michael's calls on the first of the year, and hide in your bedroom—which has not at all changed—when you see him in his Seminoles hoodie, stomping toward your house. Listen as he demands to talk to you, and your mom lies like you asked her to and says you're not home. Watch the conversation from between the blinds of the window that faces the driveway. Swallow down the wave of nausea when you catch your mother winking at him and tilting her head toward that window. Pack immediately and live out of your suitcase for the one week left in your visit.

Go play pool with Myra, one of your closest alphabetical friends and say, *Oh man, that sucks,* when she tells you she's still working as a truck dispatcher for El Dorado Furniture. She will try to ignore you by making fun of your shoes, which you bought near campus, and which you didn't like at first but now appreciate for their comfort. Say, Seriously chica, that's a high school job—you can't work there forever.

—Shut up with this chica crap like you know me, she says.

Then she slams her pool cue down on the green felt and throws the chunk of chalk at you as she charges out. Avoid embarrassment by shaking your head No as she leaves, like you regret sending her to her room with no dinner but she left you no choice. Say to the people at the table next to yours, What the fuck, huh? One guy will look down at your hippie sandals and ask, How do you know Myra? Be confused, because you and Myra always had the same friends thanks to the alphabet, but you've never in your life seen this guy before that night.

While you drive home in your mom's car, think about what happened at the pool place. Replay the sound of the cue slapping the table in your head, the clinking balls as they rolled out of its way but didn't hide in the pockets. Decide not to talk to Myra for a while, that inviting her to come visit you up north is, for now, a bad idea. Wipe your face on your sleeve before you go inside your house, and when your mom asks you why you look so upset tell her the truth: you can't believe it—Myra is jealous.

Become an RA yourself your next year so that your parents don't worry as much about money. Attend all orientation workshops and decide, after a sexual harassment prevention role-playing where Russel, another new RA, asked if *tit-fucking* counted as rape, that you will only do this for one year. Around Rush Week, hang up the anti–binge drinking posters the Hall Director put in your mailbox. On it is a group of eight grinning students; only one of them is white. You look at your residents and are confused: they are all white, except for the girl from Kenya and the girl from California. Do not worry when these two residents start spending hours hanging out in your room—letting them sit on your bed does not constitute sexual harassment. Laugh with them when they make fun of the poster. *Such Diversity in One University!* Recommend them to your Hall Director as potential RA candidates for next year.

When you call home to check in (you do this five times a week), ask how everyone is doing. Get used to your mom saying, Fine, Fine. Appreciate the lack of detail—you have limited minutes on your phone plan and besides, your family, like you, is young and indestructible. They have floated across oceans and sucker-punched sharks with their bare hands. Your father eats three pounds of beef a day and his cholesterol is fine. Each weeknight, just before crossing herself and pulling a thin sheet over her pipe-cleaner legs, your ninety-nine-year-old great-grandmother smokes a cigar while sipping a glass of whiskey and water. No one you love has ever died—just one benefit of the teenage parenthood you've magically avoided despite the family tradition. Death is far off for every Cuban—you use Castro as your example. You know everyone will still be in Hialeah when you decide to come back.

Join the Spanish Club, where you meet actual lisping Spaniards and have a hard time understanding what they say. Date the treasurer, a grad student in Spanish Literature named Marco, until he mentions your preference for being on top during sex subconsciously functions as retribution for *his* people conquering *your* people. Quit the Spanish Club and check out several Latin American history books from the library to figure out what the hell he's talking about. Do not tell your mother you broke things off; she loves Spaniards, and you are twenty and not married and you refuse to settle down.

—We are not sending you so far away to come back with nothing, she says.

At the end of that semester, look at a printout of your transcript and give yourself a high-five (to anyone watching, you're just clapping). Going home for the summer with this printout still constitutes coming back with nothing despite the good grades, so decide to spend those months working full time at the campus movie theater, flirting with sunburned patrons.

Come senior year, decide what you need is to get back to your roots. Date a brother in Iota Delta, the campus's Latino Fraternity, because one, he has a car, and two, he gives you credibility in the collegiate minority community you forgot to join because you were hiding in the library for the past three years and never saw the flyers. Tell him you've always liked Puerto Ricans (even though every racist joke your father has ever told you involved Puerto Ricans in some way). Visit his house in Cherry Hill, New Jersey, and meet his third-generation American parents who cannot speak Spanish. Do not look confused when his mother serves meatloaf and mashed potatoes and your boyfriend calls it *real home cooking.* You have only ever had meatloaf in the school dining hall, and only once. Avoid staring at his mother's multiple chins. Hold your laughter even as she claims that Che Guevara is actually still alive and living in a castle off the coast of Vieques. Scribble physical notes inside your copy of *Clarissa* (the subject of your senior thesis) detailing all the ridiculous things his mother says while you're there: taking a shower while it rains basically guarantees you'll be hit by lightning; paper cannot actually be recycled; Puerto Ricans invented the fort. Wait until you get back to campus to call your father.

After almost four years away from Hialeah, panic that you're panicking when you think about going back—you had to leave to realize you ever wanted to. You'd thank Michael for the push, but you don't know where he is. You have not spoken to Myra since the blowout by the pool table. You only know she still lives with her parents because her mom and your mom see each other every Thursday while buying groceries at Sedano's. At your Iota brother's suggestion, take a Latino Studies class with him after reasoning that it will make you remember who you were in high school and get you excited about moving back home.

Start saying things like, What does it really mean to be a minority? How do we construct identity? How is the concept of race forced upon us? Say these phrases to your parents when they ask you when they should drive up to move your stuff back to your room. Dismiss your father as a lazy thinker when he answers, What the fuck are you talking about? Break up with the Iota brother after deciding he and his organization are posers buying into the Ghetto-Fabulous-Jennifer-Lopez-Loving Latino identity put forth by the media; you earned an A- in the Latino Studies course. After a fancy graduation dinner where your mom used your hotplate to cook arroz imperial—your favorite—tell your family you can't come home, because you need to know what home means before you can go there. Just keep eating when your father throws his fork on the floor and yells, What the fuck are you talking about? Cross your fingers under the table after you tell them you're going to grad school and your mom says, But mamita, you made a promise.

Move to what you learn is nicknamed The Great White North. Tell yourself, this is America! This is the heartland! Appreciate how everyone is so *nice,* but claim Hialeah fiercely since it's all people ask you about anyway. They've never seen hair so curly, so dark. You have never felt more Cuban in your life, mainly because for the first time, you are consistently being identified as *Mexican or something.* This thrills you until the beginning-of-semester party for your grad program: you are the only person in attendance who is not white, and you're the only one under five foot seven. You stand alone by an unlit floor lamp, holding a glass of cheap red wine. You wish that Iota brother were around to protect you; he was very big; people were scared he would eat them; he had *Puro Latino* tattooed across his shoulders in Olde English Lettering. Chug the wine and decide that everyone in the world is a poser except maybe your parents. You think, *what does that even mean—poser*? Don't admit that you are somewhat drunk. Have another glass of wine and slip Spanish words into your sentences to see if anyone asks you about them. Consider yourself very charming and the most attractive female in your year, by far—you are *exotic*. Let one of the third-year students drive you home after he says he doesn't think you're okay to take a bus. Tell him, What, puta, you think I never rode no bus in Miami? Shit, I grew up on the bus. Do not tell him it was a private bus your parents paid twenty dollars a week for you to ride, along with other neighborhood kids, because they thought the public school bus was too dangerous—*they* had actually grown up on the busses you're now claiming. Your dad told you stories about bus fights, so you feel you can wing it as the third-year clicks your seatbelt on for you and says, That's fascinating—what does *puta* mean?

Spend the rest of that summer and early fall marveling at the lightning storms that you're sure are the only flashy thing about the Midwest. Take three months to figure out that the wailing sounds you sometimes hear in the air are not in your head—they are tornado sirens.

As the days grow shorter, sneak into tanning salons to maintain what you call your natural color. Justify this to yourself as healthy. You need more Vitamin D than these Viking people, you have no choice. Relax when the fake sun actually does make you brown, rather than the play-dough orange beaming off your students—you have genuine African roots! You knew it all along! Do not think about how, just like all the other salon patrons, you reek of drying paint and burnt hair every time you emerge from that ultraviolet casket.

Date the third-year because he finds you *fascinating* and asks you all sorts of questions about growing up in *el barrio*, and you like to talk anyway. More importantly, he has a car, and you need groceries, and this city is much colder than your college home—you don't plan on walking anywhere. And you are lonely. Once the weather turns brutal and your heating bill hits triple digits, start sleeping with him for warmth. When he confesses that the growth you'd felt between his legs is actually a third testicle, you'll both be silent for several seconds, then he will growl, It doesn't actually *function.* He will grimace and grind his very square teeth as if you'd just called him *Tri-Balls,* even though you only said it in your head. When he turns away from you on the bed and covers his moon-white legs, think that you could love this gloomy, deformed person; maybe he has always felt the loneliness sitting on you since you left home, except for him, it's because of an extra-heavy nut-sack. Lean toward him and tell him you don't care—say it softly, of course—say that you would have liked some warning, but that otherwise it's just another fact about him. Do not use the word *exotic* to describe his special scrotum. You've learned since moving here that that word is used to push people into some separate, freakish category.

Break up with him when, after a department happy hour, you learn from another third-year that he's recently changed his dissertation topic to something concerning the Cuban-American community in Miami. He did this a month ago—*didn't he tell you?* On the walk to the car, accuse him of using you for research purposes.

—Maybe I did, he says, But that isn't *why* I dated you, it was a *bonus.*

Tell him that being Cuban is no more a bonus than, say, a third nut. Turn on your heel and walk home in single-digit weather while he follows you in his car and yelps from the lowered window, Can't we talk about this? Call your mother after cursing him out in front of your apartment building for half an hour while he just stood there, observing.

—Oh please, she says, her voice far away, Like anyone would want to read about Hialeah.

Do not yell at your mother for missing the point.

Change advisors several times until you find one who does not refer to you as *the Mexican one* and does not ask you how your research applies to *regular* communities. Sit in biweekly off-campus meetings with your fellow Latinas, each of them made paler by the Great White North's conquest over their once-stubborn pigment. They face the same issues in their departments—the problem, you're learning, is system-wide. Write strongly worded joint letters to be sent at the end of the term. Think, *Is this really happening? I am part of this group?* Look at the dark greenish circles hanging under their eyes, the curly frizz poking out from their pulled-back hair and think, *Why did I think I had a choice?*

Call home less often. There is nothing good to report.

—Why can't you just *shut up* about being Cuban, your mother says after asking if you're still causing trouble for yourself. No one would even notice if you flat-ironed your hair and stopped talking.

Put your head down and plow through the years you have left there because you know you will graduate: the department can't wait for you to be gone. You snuck into the main office (someone had sent out an email saying there was free pizza in the staff fridge) and while your mouth worked on a cold slice of pepperoni, you heard the program coordinator yak into her phone that they couldn't wait to get rid of the troublemaker.

—I don't know, she says seconds later, Probably about spics, that's her only angle.

You sneak back out of the office and spit the pepperoni out in a hallway trashcan because you're afraid of choking—you can't stop laughing. You have not heard the word *Spic* used in the past decade. Your parents were *Spics*. *Spics* is so seventies. They would not believe someone just called you that. Crack up because even the Midwest's slurs are way behind the East Coast. Rename the computer file of your dissertation draft *Spictacular*. Make yourself laugh every time you open it.

Embrace your obvious masochism. Make it your personal mission to educate the middle of the country about Latinos by living there just a little longer. But you have to move—you can't work in a department that your protests helped to officially document as *Currently Inhospitable to Blacks and Latinos*, even if it is friendly to disabled people and people with three testicles.

Decide to stay in the rural Midwest partly for political reasons: you have done what no one in your family has ever done—you have voted in a state other than Florida. And you cannot stand Hialeah's politics. You monitored their poll results via the Internet. Days before the election, you received a mass email from

Myra urging you to vote for the candidate whose books you turn upside down when you see them in stores. Start to worry you have communist leanings—wonder if that's really so bad. Keep this to yourself; you do not want to hear the story of your father eating grasshoppers while in a Cuban prison, not again.

Get an adjunct position at a junior college in southern Wisconsin, where you teach a class called The Sociology of Communities. You have seventy-six students and, unlike your previous overly polite ones, these have opinions. Several of them are from Chicago and recognize your accent for what it actually is—not Spanish, but Urban. Let this give you hope. Their questions about Miami are about the beach, or if you'd been there during a particular hurricane, or if you've ever been to the birthplace of a particular rapper. Smile and nod, answer them after class—keep them focused on the reading.

At home, listen to and delete the week's messages from your mother. She is miserable because you have abandoned her, she says. You could have been raped and dismembered, your appendages strewn about Wisconsin and Illinois, and she would have no way of knowing.

—You would call if you'd been dismembered, right? the recording says.

It has only been eight days since you last spoke to her.

The last message you do not delete. She is vague and says she needs to tell you something important. She is crying. You call back, forgetting about the time difference—it is eleven-thirty in Hialeah.

Ask, What's wrong?

—Can I tell her? she asks your father. He says, I don't care.

—Tell me what?

Tuck your feet under you on your couch and rub your eyes with your free hand.

—Your cousin Barbarita, she says, Barbarita has a brain tumor.

Say, What, and then, Is this a fucking joke?

Take your hand away from your eyes and stick your thumbnail in your mouth. Gnaw on it. Barbarita is eleven years older than you. She taught you how to spit and how to roller-skate. You cannot remember the last time you talked to her, but that is normal—you live far away. Then it comes to you. Eight months ago, at Noche Buena, last time you were home.

—It's really bad. They know it's cancer. We didn't want to tell you.

Sigh deeply, sincerely. You expected something about your centurial great-grandmother going in her whiskey-induced sleep. You expected your father having to cut back to one pound of beef a day because of his tired heart.

Ask, Mom, you okay? Assume her silence is due to more crying. Say, Mom?

—She's been sick since February, she says.

Now you are silent. It is late August. You did not go back for your birthday this year—you had to find a job, and the market is grueling. Your mother had said she understood. Also, you adopted a rabbit in April (you've been a little lonely in Wisconsin), and your mother knows you don't like leaving the poor thing alone for too long. Push your at-the-ready excuses out of the way and say, Why didn't you tell me before?

She does not answer your question. Instead she says, You have to come home.

Tell her you will see when you can cancel class. There is a fall break coming up, you might be able to find a rabbit-sitter and get away for a week.

—No, I'm sorry I didn't tell you before. I didn't want you to worry. You couldn't do anything from up there.

Wait until she stops crying into the phone. You feel terrible—your poor cousin. She needs to get out and see the world; she has never been further north than Orlando. When she was a teenager, she'd bragged to you that one day, she'd move to New York City and never come back. You think (but know better than to say), Maybe this is a blessing in disguise. When you see her, you will ignore the staples keeping her scalp closed over her skull. You will pretend to recognize your cousin through the disease and the bloated, hospital gown–clad monster it's created. You will call her *Barbarino* like you used to, and make jokes when no one else can. Just before you leave—visiting hours end, and you are just a visitor—you'll lean in close to her face, so close your nose brushes the tiny hairs still clinging to her sideburns, and say, Tomorrow. Tomorrow I'm busting you out of here.

Your mother says, She died this morning. She went fast. The service is the day after tomorrow. Everyone else will be there, please come.

You are beyond outrage—you feel your neck burning hot. You skip right past your dead cousin and think, *I cannot believe these people. They have robbed me of my final hours with my cousin. They have robbed Barbarita of her escape.*

You will think about your reaction later, on the plane, when you try but fail to rewrite a list about the windows of your parents' house in the margins of an in-flight magazine. But right now, you are still angry at being left out. Promise your mother you'll be back in Hialeah in time and say nothing else. Hang up, and book an eight-hundred-dollar flight home after emailing your students that class is canceled until further notice.

Brush your teeth, put on flannel pajamas (even after all these winters, you are still always cold), tuck yourself in to bed. Try to make yourself cry. Pull out the ladybug-adorned to-do list pad from the milk crate you still use as a nightstand and write down everything you know about your now-dead cousin.

Here's what you remember: Barbarita loved papaya and making jokes about papaya. One time, before she even knew what it meant, she called her sister a *papayona* in front of everyone at a family pig roast. Her mother slapped her hard enough to lay her out on the cement patio. She did not cry, but she stormed inside to her room and did not come out until she'd said the word *papayona* out loud and into her pillow two hundred times. Then she said it another hundred times in her head. She'd told you this story when your parents dragged you to visit Barbarita's mom and her newly busted hip while you were home during one of your college breaks. Barbarita's mother, from underneath several white blankets, said, I never understood why you even like that fruit. It tastes like a fart.

Barbarita moved back in with her parents for good after her mom fractured her hip. The family scandal became Barbarita's special lady-friend, with whom she'd been living the previous eight years. You remember the lady-friend's glittered fanny pack—it always seemed full of breath mints and rubber bands—how you'd guessed it did not come off even for a shower. Barbarita took you to Marlins games and let you drink stadium beer from the plastic bottle if you gave her the change in your pockets. She kept coins in a jar on her nightstand and called it her retirement fund. She made fun of you for opening a savings account when you turned sixteen and said you'd be better off stuffing the cash in a can and burying it in the backyard. She laughed and slapped her knee and said, No lie, I probably have ninety thousand dollars under my mom's papaya tree.

Look at your list. It is too short. Whose fault is that? You want to say God; you want to say your parents. You want to blame the ladybug imprinted on the paper. You are jealous of how she adorns yet can ignore everything you've put down. Write, *My cousin is dead and I'm blaming a ladybug.* Cross out *my cousin* and write *Barbarita.* Throw the pad back in the crate before you write, *Am I really this selfish?*

Decide not to sleep. The airport shuttle is picking you up at 4 AM anyway, and it's already 1. Get out of bed, set up the automatic food dispenser in your rabbit's cage, then flat-iron your hair so that it looks nice for the funeral. Your father has cursed your frizzy head and blamed the bad genes on your mother's side since you sprouted the first tuft. Wrap the crispy ends of your hair around Velcro rollers and microwave some water in that I-don't-do-Mondays mug that you never use (the one you stole off the grad program coordinator's desk right before shoving your keys in the drop box—you couldn't help stealing it: you're a spic). Stir in the Café Bustelo instant coffee your mother sent you a few weeks ago in a box that also contained credit card offers you'd been mailed at their address and three packs of Juicy Fruit. The spoon clinks against the mug and it sounds to you like the slightest, most insignificant noise in the world.

Sit at the window seat that convinced you to sign the lease to this place even though your closest neighbor is a six-minute drive away. Listen to the gutters around the window flood with rain. Remember the canal across from your parents' house, how the rain threatened to flood it twice a week. There is a statue of San Lázaro in their front yard and a mango tree in the back. Lázaro is wedged underneath an old bathtub your dad half buried vertically in the dirt, to protect the saint from rain. The mango tree takes care of itself. But your father made sure both the mango tree and San Lázaro were well guarded behind a five-foot-high chain-link fence. The house's windows had bars—rejas—on them to protect the rest of his valuables, the ones living inside. You never noticed the rejas (every house around for blocks had them) until you left and came back. The last night of your first winter break in Hialeah, just before you went to sleep, you wasted four pages—front and back—in a notebook scribbling all the ways the rejas were a metaphor for your childhood: *a caged bird, wings clipped, never to fly free; a zoo animal on display yet up for sale to the highest-bidding boyfriend; a rare painting trapped each night after the museum closes.* Roll your eyes—these are the ones you remember now. You didn't mean it, not even as you wrote them, but you wanted to mean it, because that made your leaving an escape and not a desertion. Strain to conjure up more of them—it's got to be easier than reconciling the pilfered mug with your meager list about your cousin. But you can't come up with anything else. All you remember is your father weeding the grass around the saint every other Saturday, even in a downpour.

Peek through the blinds and think, *It will never stop raining.* Pack light—you still have clothes that fit you in your Hialeah closet. Open the blinds all the way and watch the steam from your cup play against the reflected darkness, the flashes of rain. Watch lightning careen into the flat land surrounding your tiny house, your empty, saint-less yard. Wait for the thunder. You know, from growing up where it rained every afternoon from three to five, that thunder's timing tells you how far you are from the storm. You cannot remember which cousin taught you this—only that it wasn't Barbarita. When it booms just a second later, know the lightning is too close. Lean your forehead against the windowpane and feel the glass rattle, feel the vibration pass into your skull, into your teeth. Keep your head down; see the dozens of tiny flies, capsized and drained, dead on the sill. Only the shells of their bodies are left, along with hundreds of broken legs that still manage to point at you. If you squint hard enough, the flies blend right into the dust padding their mass grave. And when your eyes water, even these dusty pillows blur into an easy, anonymous gray smear.

Your hands feel too heavy to open the window, then the storm glass, then the screen, to sweep their corpses away. You say out loud to no one, I'll do it when I get back. But your words—your breath—rustle the burial ground, sending tiny swirls of dust toward your face. It tastes like chalk and dirt. Feel it scratch the roof of your mouth, but don't cough—you don't need to. Clear your throat if you want; it won't make the taste go away any faster.

Don't guess how long it will take for the clouds to clear up; you're always wrong about weather. The lightning comes so close to your house you're sure this time you'll at least lose power. Close your eyes, cross your fingers behind your back. Swallow hard. The windowsill's grit scrapes every cell in your throat on its way down. Let this itch convince you that the lightning won't hit—it can't, not this time—because for now, you're keeping your promise. On the flight, distract yourself with window lists and SkyMall magazine all you want; no matter what you try, the plane will land. Despite the traffic you find worse than you remember, you'll get to Hialeah in time for the burial—finally back, ready to mourn everything.

THE IOWA SHORT FICTION AWARD AND JOHN SIMMONS SHORT FICTION AWARD WINNERS, 1970–2009

Donald Anderson
Fire Road
Dianne Benedict
Shiny Objects
David Borofka
Hints of His Mortality
Robert Boswell
Dancing in the Movies
Mark Brazaitis
The River of Lost Voices: Stories from Guatemala
Jack Cady
The Burning and Other Stories
Pat Carr
The Women in the Mirror
Kathryn Chetkovich
Friendly Fire
Cyrus Colter
The Beach Umbrella
Jennine Capó Crucet
How to Leave Hialeah
Jennifer S. Davis
Her Kind of Want
Janet Desaulniers
What You've Been Missing
Sharon Dilworth
The Long White
Susan M. Dodd
Old Wives' Tales
Merrill Feitell
Here Beneath Low-Flying Planes
James Fetler
Impossible Appetites
Starkey Flythe, Jr.
Lent: The Slow Fast
Sohrab Homi Fracis
Ticket to Minto: Stories of India and America
H. E. Francis
The Itinerary of Beggars
Abby Frucht
Fruit of the Month
Tereze Glück
May You Live in Interesting Times
Ivy Goodman
Heart Failure
Ann Harleman
Happiness
Elizabeth Harris
The Ant Generator
Ryan Harty
Bring Me Your Saddest Arizona
Mary Hedin
Fly Away Home
Beth Helms
American Wives
Jim Henry
Thank You for Being Concerned and Sensitive
Lisa Lenzo
Within the Lighted City
Kathryn Ma
All That Work and Still No Boys
Renée Manfredi
Where Love Leaves Us
Susan Onthank Mates
The Good Doctor
John McNally
Troublemakers
Molly McNett
One Dog Happy
Kevin Moffett
Permanent Visitors
Lee B. Montgomery
Whose World Is This?

Rod Val Moore
Igloo among Palms
Lucia Nevai
Star Game
Thisbe Nissen
Out of the Girls' Room and into the Night
Dan O'Brien
Eminent Domain
Philip F. O'Connor
Old Morals, Small Continents, Darker Times
Sondra Spatt Olsen
Traps
Elizabeth Oness
Articles of Faith
Lon Otto
A Nest of Hooks
Natalie Petesch
After the First Death There Is No Other
Glen Pourciau
Invite
C. E. Poverman
The Black Velvet Girl
Michael Pritchett
The Venus Tree
Nancy Reisman
House Fires
Elizabeth Searle
My Body to You
Enid Shomer
Imaginary Men
Marly Swick
A Hole in the Language
Barry Targan
Harry Belten and the Mendelssohn Violin Concerto
Annabel Thomas
The Phototropic Woman
Jim Tomlinson
Things Kept, Things Left Behind
Doug Trevor
The Thin Tear in the Fabric of Space
Laura Valeri
The Kind of Things Saints Do
Anthony Varallo
This Day in History
Don Waters
Desert Gothic
Lex Williford
Macauley's Thumb
Miles Wilson
Line of Fall
Russell Working
Resurrectionists
Charles Wyatt
Listening to Mozart
Don Zancanella
Western Electric